The Awakening

Toni Sheree

Dedication

This book is first and foremost dedicated to GOD! All of my creativity flows directly from You! I owe You, God! You get the glory for every creative idea that flows through me!

To my parents! Thank you for all that you do for me! Thank you for always encouraging my creativity. You always allowed me to express myself in whatever ways I needed to. Mom, for every journal you ever bought me! Thank you! It allowed me to become comfortable expressing myself in writing.

Last but not least, to Auntie Twyla and Uncle Dre! Thank you for constantly pouring into me over the past three years! Thank you for constantly pushing me to be a better me!

chapter one

It is Saturday evening, and James and Anna are in the driveway playing basketball. James is up 20-19.

"Game point." James says.

"Let's go old man!" Anna exclaims. Anna tries to steal the ball, but James gets around her and dunks it for the winning point.

"And the crowd goes wild!" James yells.

"Good game pops. I got you next time though." Anna says hugging her father.

"Dinner's ready!" Amie, James' youngest daughter walks outside and says.

"Heads up!" Anna yells as she throws the ball to her sister. Amie quickly dodges the ball.

"Ew!" Amie goes inside.

"How did you two become complete opposites?" James asks as they walk inside. Monica, James' wife, has the table set for dinner.

"Go wash up so we can eat." Monica says.

"Yes ma'am." Anna heads upstairs.

"Yes baby." James kisses his wife. When everyone gets to the table, they eat.

"Did dad tell you I almost beat him?" Anna asks.

"Almost, but you didn't. Maybe next time kiddo." James responds.

"I dunked on you, though!" Anna smiles.

"That was a nice dunk." James smiles back at Anna.

"But that crossover you did to win the game was hot!" Anna exclaims.

"Alright! Enough basketball talk! Amie has a ballet recital coming up." Monica interrupts.

"When?" James asks.

"I already told you a million times, daddy. It's this Friday." Amie answers.

"Oh. Anna's first practice with the boys is Friday." James responds.

"But you haven't been to any of my recitals." Amie whines.

"I'm sorry, but I have to stick to my commitment. Plus, it's not every day that your daughter is picked to practice with a men's college team." James explains. Amie and Monica roll their eyes.

"I don't see the big deal about that ugly sport. You chase people around the court and you're all smelly and nasty after." Amie says.

"And what's so special about ballet? Ugly feet?" Anna asks angrily.

"Better than looking like a boy half the time." Amie rebuttals.

"You know what-"Anna stands up.

"Both of you stop it now." Monica interjects.

"I'm leaving. I don't have time for this." Anna drops her silverware and leaves to get her things.

"Anna!" James calls out, but Anna keeps walking. James goes after Anna.

"Anna, stop. Your mother cooked dinner, so come enjoy it." James says.

"Dad! Neither Amie or mom respects me or my interests. Amie's always picking fights, and I'm just supposed to take it?"

"You're in college. She's in high school. Set the example."

"Fine dad. I've lost my appetite and I have homework. May I go now?"

"Sure honey. Just apologize to your sister."

"Fine." Anna rolls her eyes. Anna grabs her bag and goes downstairs with her dad. When they get to the table, Monica taps Amie.

"Sorry Anna." Amie says as James flicks Anna's ear.

"Sorry Amie." Anna sighs.

"Great. Now you two are sisters. Treat each other better!" Monica orders.

"Yes ma'am." They both reply. Anna hugs her mom and goes to her car with James.

"See you Friday?" Anna asks James.

"Of course! I wouldn't miss your first practice for the world."

"Love you dad."

"Love you too." Anna heads straight to her best friends room when she gets back to campus. Once she's there, she walks in his room.

"My ninja, Will!" Anna exclaims.

"One day you're gonna walk in and I'ma have a girl in here." Will responds.

"Yeah right."

"How was the crib?"

"Terrible. But, I almost whooped my dad tonight."

"You always almost whoop him."

"Shut up. Amie and I got into it again."

"Nothing new. You hungry?"

"Starving. I barely touched dinner."

"Good. I knew you'd be here soon, so I ordered us some wings."

"And that's why you're my best friend."

"You ready for practice, Friday?"

"You know it. Shout out to you for talking to coach."

"You need to join the women's team. They'd have no choice but to offer you a full scholarship."

"I'm cool on it. No way am I playing for them."

"You have what it takes to make it pro."

"I'll stick to physical therapy."

"You are so hard headed. You know pops would love to see you go pro."

"I'm not living out my dad's dream. I'm living out mine."

"Mhmmm. One day you'll listen." There's a knock at the door.

"Wings are here." A guy yells.

"Time to grub." Anna says as Will goes to get the food. Back at the Winefield household, Monica is cleaning up dinner as James watches ESPN in the kitchen.

"What are we going to do about these girls?" Monica asks.

"I don't know. They're getting out of hand." James answers.

"You and Amie need to spend more time together."

"As do you and Anna."

"I try to spend time with Anna. I invite her shopping all the time."

"Anna hates shopping."

"What girl hates shopping?"

"Our daughter."

"What about you? You haven't seen your daughter dance in years."

"Those recitals are so boring. But, I will go to a recital if you come watch Anna play."

"Anything to keep the peace." Monica kisses her husband. James grabs Monica's hand and pulls her to his lap.

"I love you, baby." James says.

"I love you too. Let's go upstairs." Monica responds. James picks his wife up and carries her upstairs.

The next morning, Anna awakens noticing she fell asleep in Will's room again.

"You might as well move in." Will says as he finishes getting dressed.

"What would your little girlfriends think?"

"That I'm a grown man and my best friend can spend the night whenever... unless we're gettin' it on."

"Eww."

"Get ready! We have chem in fifteen minutes." Will says. Anna walks across the hall to her room. She and Will live in the same co-ed dorm. Five minutes later, Anna opens the door to see Will waiting.

"Let's go!" Anna exclaims. As Anna and Will walk around campus, everyone speaks to them. Will is one of the basketball team's star players. All the guys love Anna, but the girls hate her because she's cool with all the guys.

"Here these girls go rollin' their eyes."

"They're just jealous. I mean... you are walking with the best looking guy on campus." Will laughs. Anna punches his arm laughing. When they get to class, they take their seats next to a few of Will's teammates.

"Al, Damen, Joey! Whaddup!" Anna asks. They dap Anna and Will.

"Anna! You're not scared are you?" Al asks

"Of?" Anna responds.

"Facing me in practice."

"Ha! I think you should be a comedian, not a ball player."

"Alright. Don't cry when I knock you over."

"Don't cry when I dunk on you."

"Yeah right. But on the real, you better bring it."

"Don't worry. I always do." Anna responds confidently. Class starts and everyone quiets down.

Friday comes along, and it's finally time for practice. Monica, James, and Amie drive up to the school to see Anna.

"Why did I have to come?" Amie asks as they walk to the practice gym.

"To support your sister." James responds. Amie rolls her eyes until she sees a couple cute guys. When they sit down and see Anna, they cheer. Anna waves. The family watches intently as Anna participates in various drills. She even runs with the team just to show how tough she is. They go over a few plays and end practice with a scrimmage. Anna, a point guard, faces off with Al. He does not hesitate to give her a hard time. But, Anna being the star that she is shows out with three pointer after three pointer. Anna runs the ball for the last play of the game. No one is open, so she carefully handles the ball. Suddenly, she crosses Al, and dunks the ball. Will runs around screaming with a couple other guys. He picks Anna up over his shoulder screaming.

"Al got played!" Everyone yells and laughs. Al high fives Anna when Will puts her down.

"Well played my friend." Al says to Anna.

"Thanks. You also." Anna responds. James, Monica, and Amie make their way to the court.

"Well played." James high fives and hugs his daughter.

"I didn't know you were that good, Anna. I'll have to watch you play more often." Monica adds.

"Thanks mom. Enjoy the show, squirt?" Anna asks Amie.

"It was cool, I guess. You guys smell, though. Ew." Anna just rolls her eyes.

"Come here guys. These are my parents." Anna signals to a couple of the guys.

"Hey" can be heard from the guys.

"These are my mains; Al, Joey, and Damen." Anna says.

"Pleasure to meet you young men." Monica says as James shakes their hands.

"Hey mom, pops, Amie." Will approaches them as the rest of the guy's head to the locker room.

"Will!" Monica exclaims.

"My man Will. Taking care of my little girl?" James asks.

"You know it." Will responds.

"Got any plans tonight? I made you and Anna's favorite." Monica says.

"Oh, I'm definitely gonna slide through." Will responds.

"Coach!" Anna yells.

"Anna! Great job. Way to get Al." Coach says.

"Thanks! These are my parents, James and Monica, and my sister, Amie." Anna introduces.

"Pleasure to meet you. This means so much to both Anna and me." James shakes hands with Coach.

"Well, I'm glad to have her here whipping these boys into shape. But, I must get home. The wife's waiting with dinner. See you all later." Coach runs to the locker room.

"See you coach!" Will yells as he gives Amie a big hug.

"Get off me!" Amie yells hitting Will.

"You're such a girl." Anna laughs.

"We're gonna change and meet you at home." Will says as he and Anna head to the locker rooms.

When Anna and Will get to the house, everyone sits down for dinner.

"Let's grub! Taco night!" Anna yells.

"Thanks mom." Will says to Monica.

"Amie, what happened to your recital?" Anna asks.

"It was rescheduled for next week due to a water main break." Amie responds.

"Tragic." Anna says sarcastically.

"That means daddy will be there." Amie's face lights up.

"I sure will. Wouldn't miss it for the world." James smiles at Amie.

"I guess I can come. Practice will be earlier next Friday. Will's coming too." Anna says.

"Oh yay! You guys are gonna love it." Amie cheers. Will gives Anna an evil stare.

"You have to come now." Anna whispers to Will."

"Just wait. I'ma get you back." Will whispers back.

"What are you two whispering about?" Monica asks.

"Oh nothing." Anna lies.

"How were classes this week?" Monica asks Will and Anna. Before they can respond, the phone rings.

"I'll get it." James goes to get the phone. Monica never takes her eyes off of him.

"Classes were cool." Will responds. Monica does not respond because she notices the change in James' mood as he talks on the phone.

"Alrighty then." Anna says attempting to get Monica's attention. Moments later, James comes back to the table.

"Who was it, honey?" Monica asks.

"Uhm... my commanding officer." Everyone just sits silently.

"What'd he want?" Monica asks.

"I uhm... I've been summoned to go overseas." James stutters. Everyone freezes. Monica has a hard time taking the news in.

"What?" Monica worries.

"Sgt. Phillips has taken ill, and they need me to take his place." James responds.

"Wh-when do you leave?" Monica asks.

"The car will be here at eight in the morning." James responds.

"I can't believe this." Monica says angrily. Amie runs to her room.

"How long will you be gone?" Anna asks.

"Nine months." James responds. There is another long pause.

"Can you two excuse us?" Monica asks Anna and Will. They head upstairs to Anna's room.

"I thought there were no more surprise missions." Monica says.

"They really need me. I'm the most experienced in this area."

"I don't care about that. We need you here! Call them back and tell them no."

"Look, Monica... you knew what you were getting yourself into when you married me. This is nothing new to you. I've been called on missions before-"

"How can they just call after five years? So, you're really going to go through with this?"

"Monica, it's my job! I'll be back in nine months."

"Nine long months, James. What happens if you don't come back?"

"Stop with that nonsense. Of course I'll be back."

"Easy for you to say. You don't have to sit around here waiting!"

"We've been through this before. I'm not about to argue. I told you this would happen at random before we got married. You shouldn't have married me if you're not going to support me."

15

"You're right. You'd better pray that I'm still here in nine months."

"Really Monica?" Monica doesn't respond. She just begins to cry. James attempts to comfort her, but she snatches away. James gets up and slams his chair into the table as he leaves the room.

James goes up to Amie's room.

"You alright?" James asks Amie.

"Daddy, I don't want you to go!"

"I don't want to go either, but I have to. It's my job. I'm really sorry about having to miss your recital next week."

"You mean that?"

"Of course, baby. You and Anna are my world. I'm gonna think about you every day."

"Awh, I'm gonna miss you daddy!" Amie hugs her dad.

"I'm gonna write you every day that I can."

"That'll really mean a lot."

"Wanna play a family game after I finish packing?"

"Yes!"

"Alright, I'll come get you when we're ready." James kisses his daughter's forehead and goes to Anna's room.

Anna can tell something is bothering her dad.

"Wanna suit up?" James asks Anna.

"Of course." Anna responds.

"Will, can you record it?" James asks.

"Yeah, pops." Will responds as they head to the driveway. Anna and James both play their hearts out. During the last play, James purposely slips up and lets Anna win. Anna cheers in excitement. She's never beat her dad. Will notices James let her win and smiles to himself.

"Congrats. Bring it in." James hugs his daughter.

"Want me to keep recording?" Will asks.

"Yes. Ladies and gentlemen, James and Anna checking in to let you know Anna finally beat me in a game. You got heart, kid. Keep it up. But, it probably won't happen again." James puts Anna in a headlock and messes up her hair.

"Dad!" Anna yells laughing.

"The son I never had, I love you." James kisses Anna's forehead and Will stops recording.

"I love you too, dad. You feeling better? I could tell something was bothering you."

"You've always been good at reading people. I'm good now."

"Good. Can't wait to beat you again when you get back."

"We'll see. Go wash up and we're gonna play a game in the family room."

"Okay." Anna responds as she and Will head upstairs.

"You alright?" Will asks Anna.

"I'll be fine. It's only nine months. It'll fly by."

"I admire how tough you are... for a girl, I mean."

"Thanks for being here." Will and Anna hug.

James goes inside to call his mother.

17

"Mamma."

"Hey baby. You know how late it is? The last time you called me this late, it wasn't a pleasant call."

"I have to head out in the morning. I'll be gone for nine months." There is a pause.

"Alright baby. I don't like it, but I understand you gotta do what you gotta do. Keep in touch."

"Yes ma'am."

"How'd that wife of yours take it?"

"Not too well. She's not speaking to me right now."

"Figures. I'ma pray for y'all."

"Thanks mamma. We need it."

"Well, I love you. I'll think about you every day."

"Love you too mamma." James' mother prays with him and then they hang up. James heads upstairs. When he gets there, the bedroom door is locked.

"Really Monica? I'm about to leave and you're playing games?"

"Yep. Go away."

"Well, we're about to play a game. We'd like for you to join." James offers. Monica says nothing. Giving up, James gets Amie and they head downstairs. After a couple intense rounds, everyone heads to their rooms.

When James gets upstairs, the door is still locked.

"Monica, I have to pack!" After a pause, she opens the door. He gives her an ugly look and begins to pack.

"Can you be a little quieter? I'm trying to watch television."

"Your husband's leaving and you're giving me the cold shoulder? You even threaten to leave me? We've been married twenty-five years and you're willing to throw it all away?"

"I just need time to think." Monica responds.

"I leave in the morning!" James yells and slams the closet door.

"Don't yell at me! Look! I already told you- never mind. You don't understand."

"So help me understand!"

"If you don't get it after twenty-five years, you won't get it now."

"Try me."

"I'm afraid, James!"

"Stop all the negativity. That's the last thing I need right now. I need my wife here to encourage me. You fail to realize that everything is not about you. Our daughters are doing a better job of encouraging me than you've ever done. Every time I leave, it's the same thing! How about you support your husband for once?"

"Oh, I don't support you??" Monica yells.

"No! How many games have you watched me play since we've been married? But, you were at every game when you thought I was on my way to the NBA in college." James yells back.

"I'm so done with you right now! Get out!"

"You're kicking me out of my room?"

"Yes! Now go! Maybe we'll talk in the morning."

"It's like that?"

"Maybe we can finish in nine months." Monica says. James is appalled at what Monica just said. He grabs his things and takes them downstairs. Not wanting to sleep, he goes to Anna's room.

"You sleep?" James peaks in.

"Almost." Anna barely gets out.

"Okay. Good night baby." James says uneasy. Noticing the tone of James' voice, Anna jumps up.

"Dad wait! Let's watch our favorite movie."

"Sounds good. Meet you downstairs." James goes to get Amie.

"Will, you wanna come?" Anna asks.

"Yeah!" Will gets off the floor and they head downstairs. Will stretches out on the couch and James sits in the middle of the love seat with his feet up. Anna and Amie lay on either side of his chest as they watch their favorite movie.

Everyone but James and Anna fall asleep.

"I heard you and mom arguing. Is everything okay?" Anna asks

"Don't worry about a thing. We'll be okay. Keep your eye on your mother and sister for me while I'm gone."

"I will." They both doze off. Around six AM, James receives a call. His officer informs him that he has to leave in an hour. He wakes Will and the girls up.

"I'll be leaving earlier than I thought. The car will be here in an hour." James says. James gets dressed as Anna fixes him a quick breakfast. Once he is dressed, he goes to the bedroom, but the door is still locked. Seven o'clock is nearing, so he writes Monica a note and slides it under the door. James then goes downstairs to eat. As he is finishing up, the doorbell rings. Anna answers it.

"Commander Kelly." Anna salutes him.

"Anna! How are you?"

"I'm fine. Thank you. Come in. He's almost ready."

"Commander Kelly! Amie salutes and hugs him.

"Are you leaving also?" Anna asks.

"Yes ma'am. Your dad and I will be working together the whole time."

"Keep an eye on him for me." Anna responds.

"Will do." Commander Kelly responds.

"Jim!" James exclaims.

"James. Ready?"

"Uh. Give me a second."

"I'll take your bag." Jim hugs the girls and heads outside with James' bag.

"I guess this is it. I promise to write you two every chance I get! Be good and keep an eye on each other and your mother. That goes for you too, Will."

"Yes sir!" Will hugs James. Amie holds her dad extra tight as she begins to cry. Then Anna hugs her dad extra tight and kisses him. They watch James as he gets in the car and takes off. Amie runs to her room crying.

"You okay Anna?" Will asks. Anna grabs Will and hugs him extra tight. A few tears slide down, but she doesn't let Will see. After a few minutes, she let's go and they clean the kitchen before heading back to school.

Anna goes to her room to get her bag. On her way downstairs, she stops in Amie's room.

"You alright, squirt?" Anna asks.

"Did he have to go?"

"Yes. You were ten the last time he left. He wrote every day. It was like he was never gone."

"Really?"

"Yes! The time is gonna go by so fast. Just keep yourself busy. You should write him today and send it out. It'll mean a lot to him."

"I think I'll do that. Thanks Anna." The sisters hug. Anna tries to go downstairs, but Monica comes out of her room.

"Where's your father?" Monica asks.

"Good morning to you too. He left already."

"What?" Monica asks angrily. Anna notices the note on the floor and hands it to Monica.

"He left this for you. Commander Kelly came an hour early." Anna says. Monica snatches the note from Anna.

"I can't believe this." Monica says quietly.

"Yeah, well, Will and I are leaving. Love you."

"Love you too." Monica barely gets out. Anna and Will leave as Monica reads the letter.

"Dear Monica, I tried to say a proper goodbye, but you locked me out again. I love you and I'll think about you every day. I'll be writing and I hope you write back. I apologize for anything I said that was out of line last night. Love you, James"

22

"No. No. No." Monica says as she runs downstairs searching for James. She opens the front door hoping he's not really gone. When reality hits Monica, she runs to her room and cries.

chapter two

Will and Anna go for a walk when they get back to campus.

"Is mom alright?" Will asks.

"I have no idea. I've never heard them argue like that. I mean, they've argued every time he had to leave, but not like that."

"That's crazy. Look who it is." They look up and see the girls' basketball captain approaching them.

"Whhyyy?" Anna whines.

"Anna! Will! Hey!" Amber says excitedly.

"Amber. How are you?" Anna asks.

"Wonderful. How about you?" Amber responds.

"I'm okay. What's going on?" Anna asks.

"Well, the team is throwing a party tonight, and we'd love for you to grace us with your presence."

"Free booze?" Will asks.

"Well of course." Amber flirts.

"We'll be there! Will answers for Anna.

"Great. Bring your teammates, Will." Amber walks away.

"I can't tell if she wants you or me more." Anna laughs.

"You know you love this attention. I don't see why you don't give the team a chance. You'll be the team's star player. You'll get picked up by the WNBA so fast."

"Even if there was a chance of me joining, those chances are gone since my dad isn't here."

"I'm just saying, give it a chance. Just really put some thought to it. Try-outs are in two weeks. Just show up and show out."

"Can we drop the subject forever if I show up?"

"Yes!"

"Fine. I'll go to tryouts. But, I'm not joining."

"I can deal."

"Let's go figure out what I'm wearing tonight." Anna and Will go to her room

Will goes through Anna's closet and picks out a few outfits.

"Gotta show those curves off." Will says.

"You can put all those dresses back. I'll wear the shorts."

"With the shirt showing all your goodness?" Will laughs.

"That's the one." Anna laughs.

"Good choice."

26

"Hungry?"

"Starving."

"I brought back tacos."

"Yes! Let's grub!" Will exclaims. They eat and fall asleep in Anna's bed. Around eight, Al comes in Anna's room and dives on the bed. Anna jumps up.

"Al! Don't break my bed with your 6'7 self!" Anna yells.

"Y'all been sleep all afternoon. Get dressed so we can pregame in Joey's room."

"Alright." Will responds as Al walks out. Anna bumps music as she and Will get dressed. Once Anna's hair is curled and makeup is done, they head to Joey's room.

"Ooo wee! I knew Anna was gon kill the game tonight." Al shouts as he checks her out.

"I try." Anna laughs. They all take shots and head to the party.

As soon as they walk in the party, the girls' team is all over Anna. They take her straight to the VIP section. Anna tries to grab Will, but it's too late.

"Here's a shot, Anna." Amber hands Anna the shot.

"Thanks." Anna downs it.

"Where's Will- I mean the boys?"

"Out there. You can go get them." Anna responds pointing to the crowd of people on the dance floor. Amber goes to get the boys. Will is in a trance when he sees Amber.

"Hey boys. Wanna come to the VIP?"

"Yeah. Let's go." Will checks Amber out as she leads the way. When Al sees Anna, he approaches her.

"I've never seen you dress like this." Al says.

"You like?" Anna flirts

"Yes ma'am."

"Oh! This is my jam!" Anna gets hype.

"Wanna dance?"

"I thought you'd never ask." Anna breaks it down on Al. She looks to her left and sees Amber all over Will.

By the end of the night, everyone is beyond drunk. As they head back to the dorms, Al carries Anna on his back. Al opens Anna's door and lays her on the bed. Will goes straight to his room leading Amber to his bed.

"Hold on. Let me check on Anna." Will barely gets out because he's so drunk. Amber rolls her eyes. Will goes to Anna's door, "You got her, Al?"

"Yes. Now, go have fun." Al orders.

"Just watch her. She's going through a lot. Don't do anything she's not ready for."

"I like her too much for that. Now go. Amber's waiting on you." Will goes to his room and locks the door. Al closes and locks Anna's door.

"Was that Will?" Anna asks.

"Yeah, he was just checking on you."

"Come to bed."

"I don't mind sleeping on the floor." Al says earnestly.

"No! I wanna cuddle." Anna says. Al gets in bed and Anna kisses him on the cheek. Shortly after, they both fall asleep.

Al wakes up before Anna and watches her sleep. Anna awakens to Al and smiles.

"What time is it?" Anna asks

"Eleven. Good morning, beautiful."

"Morning. Did we...?"

"No. We just cuddled. You were too cute. Kissed me on my cheek before you fell asleep."

"I can be a fruitcake." Anna giggles.

"Wanna clean up and meet in thirty for breakfast?"

"Sounds good." Al heads down the hall to his room. Anna showers and then goes to Will's room to get her tooth brush. As she approaches his door, Amber walks out.

"Hey Amber. Is he sleep?" Anna asks.

"Yeah." Amber answers awkwardly.

"Breathe. Will is a grown man. He's free to do what he pleases. I just came to get my toothbrush. Word of advice, don't leave. Wait for him to wake up. He likes that. He'll probably ask you to breakfast."

"Thanks?" Amber follows Anna into the room. Anna grabs her toothbrush and jumps on Will's bed.

"You have company. Wake your big head up!" Anna yells.

"Get out Anna!" Will tries to grab her. Anna smiles at Amber and runs out. Will smiles as soon as he sees Amber.

"Good morning sunshine." Will says.

"Hey."

"Wanna go to breakfast?"

"Yeah. But, I need to shower."

"You can shower here. I have some sweats for you."

"Great." While Amber showers in Will's bathroom, Will walks to Anna's room.

"Have fun last night?" Will asks.

"I should be asking you that. I went straight to sleep. You invite her to breakfast?"

"Yep."

"You really like her."

"There's potential."

"Good. She's good for you." Anna assures Will. Al walks to the door.

"My man." Al daps Will.

"Whaddup." Will responds

"Ready?" Al asks Anna.

"Yep. Let's go." Anna answers. Will gives Anna a surprised look as she heads out with Al. Instead of eating on campus, Al takes Anna to a nearby restaurant for breakfast.

"I wasn't too bad last night, was I?" Anna asks.

"Well..."

"Oh gosh. I never drink that much... or at all."

"We all had way too much. I was out of it, too. I'm glad the party was on campus. Driving was definitely out of the question. But uh... I didn't know you could dance like that girl."

"Let's just say I spent a lot of time in my room practicing since the girls never liked me." Anna and Al both laugh.

"So, Will told me you're going through a lot. Anything you care to share?" Al asks changing the mood of the conversation.

"Oh Will." Anna says angrily.

"He was just looking out for you last night."

"Well, my dad went overseas yesterday morning. He'll be gone for nine months."

"Sorry to hear that. If you ever need a shoulder to lean on, I'm here."

"Thanks. You know... you're such a sweetheart. I never would've guessed."

"That's what you bring out of me. I never thought you'd give me a shot. That's why I'm always picking on you."

"Well, I've set you up for a nice play. Use it well. Who knows what'll happen."

"Alright. I take on the challenge."

"What do you have planned today?"

"You tell me."

"I'm supposed to do homework with Will, but it looks like he has his hands full." Anna says as Will and Amber walk in.

"So, is that an invitation over?"

"Yes it is."

"Fancy seeing you here." Will says as he and Amber pass by the table.

"You also." Anna responds. The waitress comes to take their orders. Once they finish eating, Al and Anna leave the restaurant.

When they get to campus, Al grabs his books and meets Anna in her room. Anna gets comfortable on her bed as Al goes through her music.

"Let's see if you have good taste in music." Al smiles. A few minutes later, Al selects a playlist and makes himself comfortable on Anna's bed. Before starting her homework, Anna writes a letter to James.

Dear Dad:

You've only been gone for twenty-four hours and I miss you like crazy. You said you'd write me, but I couldn't wait that long. I hope all is well with you. Don't be too hard on em. Tell Commander Kelly I said hi. So, guess what? Due to Will's nagging, I've decided to go to the girls' basketball team tryouts. I really wish you were here to see them. As farfetched as the idea is, if I did decide to join, what do you think? I'll be honest and say I don't want to join because you're not here. But, if you give me the okay, I'll consider it. Well, I love you dad. Write back soon.

Love Anna.

"You alright?" Al asks noticing Anna is zoned out.

"Yeah. Just wrote my dad a letter. I really miss him."

"Can I read it?"

"Sure. Go ahead." There are a few moments of silence.

"I say you should."

"Huh?"

"Join the team."

"Not you too!"

"You're practicing with a D1 men's team. You're made for pro ball."

"While this may be true, my dad's not here. He taught me everything I know. It won't be the same without him."

"I think you'd make his whole life if you joined. Just think about it."

"Fine." Anna sighs. She lays her head on Al's lap as she reads a book for class. He sets his laptop next to him as he does homework on it.

Will comes in a couple hours later.

"I see I've been replaced." Will laughs.

"You replaced me first. How was your date?" Anna asks.

"It was ight." Will answers.

"Go ahead and front while Al's here. We'll talk." Anna says.

"Goodness woman. It was nice."

"Go get your homework and come join us." Anna says.

"Ight." Will goes to get his books.

Two weeks pass and Anna is lying in Al's bed on a Saturday afternoon waiting for him to get back from the store. Someone knocks.

"Come in." Anna responds.

"Anna." Will walks in.

"Hey Will."

"I stopped by the post office and checked our mail. Here you go." Will hands Anna a letter. Her face lights up as she tears it open and begins reading.

You have no idea how much your letter meant to me. I miss you more than words could express. Everything is going well out here. I had to whip the soldiers into shape, but everything's flowing well now. How's school? I hope practice has been going well. I'm ecstatic that you're going to try out. When you make it, I really hope you accept the offer. You just don't know how much I'd love that. But, don't join simply because Will and I want you to. Join because you want to. Live out your dream. Not mine or anyone else's. Oh yeah, Commander Kelly sends his love. He's watching me tear up as I write this. I love you, baby. Keep in touch.

Love you, dad

A few tears hit the paper.

"You alright?" Will asks.

"Yeah. My dad is absolutely amazing." Anna says as Al walks in.

"You crying?" Al asks.

"No! My allergies are just bothering me." Anna lies. Al gives Anna a straight face.

"So, what'd it say?" Will asks.

"He just responded to what I sent two weeks ago... guess what! I'm going to join the team!" Anna yells.

"Forreal?" Al swings Anna around.

"Yes!" Anna says as Al puts her down. She quickly kisses him for the first time. Al is shocked. Will punches Anna's shoulder.

34

"About time." Will grabs Anna and runs down the hall screaming. People open their doors looking.

"What's going on?" Joey asks. Will runs to Joey's door and puts Anna down.

"I'm joining the women's team." Anna exclaims.

"So that means no more busting Al's butt?" Joey asks.

"Nope. Not until after the season." Anna high fives Joey and then walks back to Al's room.

"You ready to explain?" Al asks as Anna closes his door.

"I just got a letter from my dad. He loves the idea of me joining the team."

"No. The kiss."

"Oh. That." Anna responds embarrassed.

"Yeah that." Al laughs.

"I've wanted to do it for two weeks! I felt that was the perfect moment."

"Well-" Before Al can finish his statement, Anna jumps in his arms and kisses him. Suddenly, Al's door swings open and Anna awkwardly jumps off of him. They stare at the door awkwardly.

"I didn't interrupt anything, did I?" Joey asks.

"No. Wassup?" Al asks.

"Party tonight at the loft." Joey says.

"We in there." Al daps Joey.

"Ight. Pregame in Damen's room." Joey informs them.

"We'll be there." Al says as Joey leaves.

"Ready for another crazy night?" Anna asks.

"The question is are you ready?" Al chuckles.

"Well of course! I'm gonna go start getting ready."

"Alright beautiful." Al smiles. Anna smiles back at Al and leaves.

Anna goes to Will's room.

"You going to the party?" Anna asks.

"You know it. Your room or mine?"

"Yours. Let me get my outfit and I'll be back." As tradition holds, Anna and Will get ready together. Anna finishes her hair and makeup and they head to Damen's room. Everybody takes shots and heads to the party. As soon as they walk in, Will sees Amber. She sees him, smiles and waves. He nods at her.

"Now y'all act like y'all don't know each other." Anna says to Will. Will just shrugs. Al and Anna are around each other the whole night. Neither has a desire to dance with anyone else. As always, the girls' team is all over Anna because they really want her on the team. By the end of the night, everyone is completely drunk. Al gives Anna a piggy back ride back to the dorm. Will is walking with teammates until a few girls approach them.

"What y'all getting into?" A girls asks Will.

"Heading to bed, I guess." Will responds.

"Want some company?" The girl asks.

"Well of course." Will, Joey, and Damen all smirk at each other and head to the dorm with their girls.

Anna and Al go straight to Al's room. Ann starts undressing and puts one of Al's t-shirts on. Al really wants to look, but he respects her privacy.

"Have fun tonight?" Al asks.

"Of course. I was with you." Anna walks up to him and they put their arms around each other. They kiss and get in bed.

"I'm so drunk right now." Anna giggles.

"You? Me too. I have a question."

"What is it?"

"Are you a virgin?"

"Why yes I am. Are you?"

"Well... no. Any particular reason you're waiting?"

"Waiting on the right one to give it to. And, my granny always stressed abstinence until marriage. She'd be pissed if she found out I was drunk or even in the same bed as you."

"Well, that's good."

"I can hear her giving me her speech. 'Now Anna, don't you be drinking and having sex. Remember what the Word says.'" Anna mimics her granny.

"Sounds like you have a loving granny."

"I do. She's amazing. But, if you have a problem waiting, let me know now."

"I don't mind waiting for you, Anna." They cuddle until they fall asleep.

That morning, Anna wakes up around six AM and can hear noises in the hallway. She peeks out of Al's door and sees a girl leaving Will's room.

"See ya." Anna says to embarrass her. Anna closes the door and gets back in bed. A couple hours later, both Al and Anna wake up.

"Morning sunshine." Al smiles.

"Hey. What are you doing today?"

"No homework to do today, so nothing planned."

"Wanna come home?"

"Home? Where your family lives?" Al asks nervously.

"Yes silly. I want you to meet my mom. Plus, I need to check on her and I don't wanna go alone."

"What about Will?"

"I want to go with you!" Anna gets aggravated.

"That's all you had to say. I'd love to go. I'll even drive."

"You were driving anyways." Anna laughs.

"When are we leaving?"

"Thirty minutes."

"Okay. Let's do it." They both shower and head out.

When they pull up to Anna's house, Anna sluggishly gets out of Al's truck.

"Nice house." Al says.

"Thanks. You ready?" Anna asks.

"Nope. But, let's go." Al smiles. Anna walks in the house with Al following her. They go straight to the kitchen.

"Anna!" Amie jumps in her sister's arms.

"Hey squirt." Anna responds confused.

"I'm so glad you're here! Take me back to school with you!" Amie says dramatically.

"Mom's that bad?"

"Yes!!" Amie yells.

"Oh lord. Remember Al?"

"I do. I'm Amie." Amie introduces herself.

"Nice to meet you, Amie." Al responds.

"Mom here?" Anna asks.

"She's in her room."

"Let's go. I'll give you a tour, Al." Anna shows Al the whole house and stops at Monica's room. She knocks.

"Come in." Monica says through the door.

"I hope you're presentable. I have company." Anna and Al walk in.

"Hey Anna!" Monica jumps up to hug her daughter.

"You remember Al?"

"Yes. The young man on the basketball team. Nice to officially meet you." Monica says.

"You also." Al responds.

"How have you been, mom?" Anna sits on the bed.

"I've been alright. Al, have a seat." Monica points to her vanity chair.

"Just alright?"

"Yes. Just alright. Missing your father."

"You should write him."

"I'm waiting on him to write me. Have you received anything from him?"

"Uhmm... no ma'am." Anna lies feeling bad for her mother.

"I suppose you're right. I'll write him one day next week."

"So... I think I might join the basketball team."

"Really? That's good, dear."

"I hope you and Amie can make it out to my games."

"Give me a game schedule, and we'll see." Monica says. Hurt by that response, Anna is ready to go.

"Well, Al and I have homework to do. I'll be back over next week." Anna lies again.

"Okay dear." Monica hugs Anna and they head downstairs closing Monica's door behind them.

"I'm out squirt." Anna says to Amie. Amie can tell Anna is upset.

"See! She's not the same! Take me with you!"

"I'll come get you for a weekend. Text me. I need to get outta here. Go stay with granny or friends. She won't even notice."

"I think I will. Thanks. See you, sis." Amie says as Anna and Al head out.

They get to Al's truck and take off.

"You alright?" Al asks. Anna doesn't respond right away. He looks at her and notices she's crying.

"I'm just so sick of my mom not supporting me. I say I'm joining a college team and she says she'll see what she can do? My first practice with you guys was her first time ever seeing me play. I just can't do this with her anymore." Anna expresses. Al grabs Anna's hand and kisses it.

"It'll be fine. She'll realize she's missing out. She's gonna come around."

"I hope so. I really don't know how much more disappointment I can take from her."

"I understand. But, I know everything is going to work out."

"Thanks babe. And don't you ever tell anyone you saw me cry!" Anna dries her tears and grabs Al's hand again.

"This is what I'm here for. And I won't. I wanna take you somewhere." All pulls up to this place off the water.

"What's this?"

"This is where I come to clear my head."

"This is beautiful. Why'd you bring me to your secret spot?"

"Because I really like you and I want to share with you a part of my life that no one else knows about." Al smiles. Anna hugs him tightly. Al kisses her forehead and they both bask in the moment.

chapter three

The next day, after a long day of classes, Anna heads to the gym for tryouts. Word that she's trying out got around the school and a lot of people show up to watch. As Anna walks to the bench to lace her shoes, she looks around for Al in the stands. Once she spots him, she is bombarded by the girls' team.

"We're so glad you decided to join us." Amber says.

"We just know coach is going to pick you." Carly, another girl on the team says.

"Thanks guys. Can I lace my shoes up?" Anna responds.

"Sorry. We'll start in about ten minutes." Amber says as they walk away. Before putting her shoes on, Anna walks to Al, Will, and the rest of the team.

"Glad y'all came!" Anna exclaims.

"You just better kill it. I wanna see you knock some girls over." Joey laughs.

"Don't I always kill it?" Anna asks as she high fives Joey.

"Good luck best friend." Will hugs Anna.

"Thanks Will."

"You nervous?" Will asks.

"A little. But, I'll get over it." Anna looks at Al.

"I'm screaming like a girl every time you make a three." Al says.

"That's gonna be a lot of screaming. I'm glad you came." Anna smiles.

"I wouldn't dare miss this. I'm your number one fan." Al smiles.

"All the cake in the air." Will laughs.

"Shut up. You know you wish Amber was over here so you could cake too!" Anna exclaims. Everybody laughs.

"Whatever." Will says.

"I'm just messin' bro. Welp, I guess I better finish getting ready." Anna turns around to walk away, but turns back around and kisses Al. All the guys start screaming.

"What was that for?" Al asks quietly. This is the first time they've kissed in public.

"Good luck." Anna smiles and walks away.

Coach walks in and starts tryouts which consist of a scrimmage. The coach puts Anna in, and Anna goes to work. As the coach observes Anna, she notices how quick of a thinker she is and how she puts plays together. Anna is killing it making three pointer after three pointer. She also assists some great shots. After subbing all the girls trying out in, coach ends tryouts. As Anna takes her shoes off and cools down, coach pulls her to her office.

"Have a seat please, Anna." Coach says.

"What's up Coach?"

"You know I've wanted you on my team since last year. Had I known about you when you were in high school, I'd have been all over you. I think you have a level of talent not too many girls have. I mean you practice with a men's team. I usually don't do things like this, but I want you for a full ride. If you continue to play until your senior year, I don't think you'll have any problems getting picked up by the WNBA. So, what do you say, Anna? We really need you." Coach persuades. Anna thinks for a few moments.

"I'm in coach!" Anna smiles.

"I'm so glad to have you! I'll allow you to have one more practice with the men's team tomorrow. But, I'll be expecting you at practice the next day at six PM sharp."

"I'll be there." They shake hands and Anna heads out to the gym.

Al, Joey, Will, and the rest of the team are waiting on Anna.

"Sooo?" Will asks in suspense.

"I'm sorry guys, I won't be busting your butts at practice anymore because I MADE IT!!" Anna yells. Everyone starts cheering. Al picks Anna up and swings her around.

"Congrats babe." He kisses her. Will then high fives her.

"Full ride?" Will asks.

"Yep."

"Told you!" I say we have a celebration dinner." Will offers.

"Let's do it." Al agrees.

"Can I shower first?" Anna asks.

"Hurry up and let's go." Will says. Al drives Anna back to the dorm.

"How you feeling?" Al asks.

"This feels like a dream. My dad's gonna be so proud of me!"

"Yeah he is. I'm proud of you also."

"Really?"

"Yes. Now hurry up. I'm starving." Al lies in Anna's bed as she hops in the shower. Once she's done, she throws some sweats and one of Al's t-shirts on.

"Let's go. You better be clean." Anna walks over to the bed. Al pulls her in the bed and kisses her.

"That's my response to the kiss you gave me in the gym."

"I couldn't have asked for a better one." Anna smiles

"Oh yeah?" He kisses her again.

"Everyone's waiting on us." Anna giggles.

"Let them wait." Al says. Suddenly, Will swings Anna's door open.

"Let's go love birds." Will says.

"We're coming." Al yells.

"Told ya." Anna kisses Al and gets up.

At the restaurant, Anna rests on Al the whole time.

"I never thought I'd see the day Anna got soft." Joey says.

"I agree." Damen cosigns.

"Aint nobody soft. Bet I dunk on you if we went one on one." Anna says.

"Is that a challenge?" Joey asks.

"Tomorrow before practice." Anna challenges.

"It's on." Joey accepts.

"Al done got soft too." Will adds.

"It be like that sometimes. Maybe y'all need to find someone worth settling down with too. Might change your life." Al says.

"Touché." Joey responds. When the food comes out, they eat and head back to campus.

Once back on campus, Al and Anna head straight to Anna's room

"So, I'm someone you'd settle down with?" Anna asks.

"Huh?"

"At the table you told the guys to find someone they'd settle down with."

"I did say that, didn't I? Yes you are. On the real, I've never felt this way about anyone."

"Really?"

"Can I be honest with you?"

"Of course."

"Us sleeping in the same bed almost every night for the past couple of weeks without having sex is out of character for me. There was once a time that if I didn't get some on the first night, we didn't see each other anymore. I really, really like you, Anna. You've taken one of the team's biggest players and made him soft, and I'm 100% okay with it."

"Wow is all I can say. I really needed to hear that." Anna turns out the lights and gets in bed.

"Good night babe."

"Nighty night." Anna holds Al's hand until she falls asleep.

The next day, the couple heads to class together. Instead of paying attention, Anna writes her dad a letter.

Dear Dad:

Sooooo... guess what?? I MADE THE TEAM!!! Coach offered me the point guard position on spot for a full ride! I really wish you could be here for our first game in one month. It's not the same without you. Mom's been acting so different. I almost don't like going home. I really hope these next eight months fly by. One last thing, I've been talking to someone. His name is Alvin, but we call him Al. He's the starting point guard on the men's team. We really like each other. So, I wanted to let you know what's up before we actually start a relationship. Well, how are you? I really miss you dad! Love you, Anna."

One tear slides down Anna's face as she folds and seals the letter. Al notices and grabs Anna's hand. After class, Anna goes straight to the post office to mail the letter. Really missing her father, she goes to her room to watch the video of their last one-on-one game. Anna watches the last play intently and notices James let her win. She rewinds it multiple times to be sure. Randomly, Will walks in.

"OMG! He let me win!" Anna yells at Will.

"What?" Will asks confused.

"The game you recorded. My dad let me win. What a jerk!"

"Oh that. Calm down. He did it for you."

"That's why he's a jerk. Why is he so sweet? I really miss him." Anna begins to cry. Will sits on the bed to comfort Anna.

"I know you do. He'll be back in no time and then you can beat him fair and square."

"I don't know what I'd do without you. You're seriously the greatest best friend ever. I love you."

"I love you too, Anna. Now, suck it up. No more crying. I don't like it." Will pops Anna's head and runs.

"I'm gonna get you punk!" Anna yells laughing hysterically.

The next day, Anna goes to her first practice with the girls. When she gets there, everyone introduces themselves.

"Nice to meet you all." Anna responds to all the introductions. As they run through drills and run, other girls are jealous because Anna seems to accomplish everything with ease. Once practice is over, Amber approaches Anna as she changes her shoes.

"Great practice, Anna." Amber says.

"Thanks Amber."

"What are you about to get into?"

"Probably go eat with the boys."

"Is Will gonna be there?"

"You wanna come?" Anna smirks.

"Uhm... I'd love to."

"Good. Just you." Anna gets up.

"Where?"

"I don't know. Come on."

Amber grabs her duffel bag and follows Anna.

"Can I ask you a question?"

"Go ahead."

"I heard Will took someone else to his room after the last party. Did he?"

"Pause! I've never had too many girlfriends, so I don't know what set of rules y'all play by. But, I don't tell my bros. business. Especially my best friend. If you're following along to get information out of me, you can step."

"I'm sorry. I didn't mean to cross any boundaries. You are definitely of a different breed, Anna." Amber apologizes.

"Thanks. Been hearing that all of my life." Anna responds with an attitude.

When they get to Anna's floor, the guys are waiting on her.

"Ready Anna... and Amber?" Joey asks loud enough for Will to hear from his room.

"Anna!" Anna hears her name being yelled from Will's room.

"I'll be right back." Anna says as she walks to his room.

"What's she doing here?" Will asks Anna.

"She asked to come. She wants to see you, Will." Anna answers.

"Really?" Will asks flattered.

"Yes. Now, let's go!" Anna goes to the hall and sees Al talking to Amber. Anna doesn't like this at all.

"Y'all ready?" Will yells to all the guys.

"What's going on here?" Anna approaches Al and Amber.

"I was just speaking." Amber answers.

"Oh. Let's go." Anna walks to Al's truck without speaking to him. Will walks up to Al and Amber.

"Well, hello there." He says to Amber.

"Hey Will." Amber blushes.

"Ready to go?"

"Yep." Amber responds as Will walks her to his car. Al walks to his truck and sees Anna waiting on him. He unlocks the doors, but she gets in without allowing him to open her door.

"What was that about" Al asks.

"I just don't trust her. What'd she say to you?"

"She just said hello and asked how I was. Why'd you bring her if you don't trust her?"

"She was asking questions about Will's whereabouts on the way here. I don't like that. Don't use me to get to somebody." Anna says with an attitude.

"I understand, but calm down. It's me."

"I'm sorry. Let's start over." Anna takes a deep breath.

"Yes. Let's do that. Hey babe. How was practice?"

"Practice was cool. I dominated every drill. How was yours?"

"I dunked on Joey."

"Haha. I'm proud of you, babe." Anna kisses him at a red light. Everyone has a good time at the restaurant and then head back to the dorms.

Over the next couple of weeks, Anna keeps practicing and getting to know the girls. She gets close enough to Amber to keep an eye on her. But, the girls she bonds with the most are Jenna and Casey. One day after practice, Anna invites Jenna and Casey to the room to study. After a while of studying, Will walks in.

"Hey Will." Anna exclaims.

"Aye. Hello ladies." Will playfully flirts.

"This is Jenna and you know Casey. Jenna, this is my best friend, Will." Anna introduces.

"I see you all the time, but we've never spoken to each other." Jenna says.

"You the new girl?" Will asks Jenna.

"Yeah, I am." Jenna giggles.

"Nice to meet you. Look what I have." Will says as he pulls a letter out of his pocket.

"You're so clutch!" Anna takes the letter from him and excitedly rips it open.

Dear Anna:

You have no idea how proud of you I am right now. I know you're going to do great this season. Now, I know you haven't been to the house in a while, so you should call and invite your mother and sister to a game. As far as this Al kid goes, tell him to keep his hands to himself. He will receive a full interrogation from me as soon as I return. I know you're going to make wise decisions, so have fun... but not too much fun. Commander Kelly and the troops are great. We made you a video yesterday. You should receive it soon. Send Will my love. I love you so much, baby.

Love, dad.

A huge smile comes to Anna's face as she finishes the letter.

"From your dad?" Jenna asks.

"Yes ma'am. He sends his love, Will." Anna responds.

"Next time you write him, tell him hi for me." Will says.

"I sure will." Anna responds.

"So, you ready to kill it in your first game?" Will pumps Anna up.

"You know it! Only two more days! Got my team with me! We all gone take heads at the game!" Anna yells. They all start cheering.

Two nights later, it's game night. The stands are filled with people eager to see Anna and the girls win. Anna runs out with the team and looks around in shock. She cannot believe all these people are here to see her team play. Will, Al, and the rest of the men's team are sitting right behind the bench. Anna looks at Al nervously, and he gives her a thumbs up. That gesture alone gives Anna a huge boost of confidence. The announcers call out the starters, and everyone begins cheering when he calls out Anna's name.

"Game time!" She says as she runs to the court high fiving her teammates. Right before the game starts, Anna scans the crowd. To her surprise, Monica and Amie are in the stands. Finally, the game starts and Anna plays her heart out. The crowd goes wild as Anna makes three pointer after three pointer. She even plays part in a lot of great assists. By the time the buzzer runs out in the second half, Anna has 31 points, 10 rebounds, and 11 assists. The girls shake hands with their competitors and head to the locker room.

As Anna walks back into the gym, the men's team starts yelling her name and cheering. She looks to Jenna and Casey in shock.

"You deserve this, girl." Jenna affirms.

"Thanks guys!" Anna yells.

"May I please have your autograph?" Al approaches Anna.

"Anna Winefield is not signing autographs tonight, but she is giving out kisses." Anna kisses Al.

"I better be the only one getting these free kisses." Al laughs. Monica and Amie approach Anna and Al.

"Mom! I'm so glad you came!" Anna exclaims.

"I had to be here. Way to play your heart out." Monica responds.

"Thanks. Hey squirt." Anna says to Amie.

"Hey Anna. Good game. Hey Al." Amie says.

"Hello there Amie and Mrs. Winefield."

"I saw the kiss. So, you two are pretty serious? My Anna doesn't kiss or bring anyone home." Monica jumps right to the chase.

"Uhmm-"Anna begins.

"Yes we are, ma'am. I really like Anna and with your permission, I'd like to really pursue her." Al responds.

"You seem like a nice young man. You have my permission. I'd like for the two of you to come to the house for dinner Friday." Monica says.

"Yes ma'am. We'll be there." Al answers.

"Your grandmother will be there." Monica tells Anna.

"Granny's gonna be at the house?" Will asks walking into the conversation.

"Hey Will. You're more than welcome to join us." Monica says.

"I'm there." Will hugs Monica and Amie.

"You're gonna be a third wheel." Amie says to Will.

"False. While Anna's with Al, I'll be playing Granny in spades."

"Well, we've got to get going. See you all Friday." Monica hugs Anna and heads to the car.

"Why is she being so nice?" Anna asks Amie.

"She's been nice for the past couple days. I think she and daddy have been talking." Amie responds.

"Finally. Alright, see you squirt." Anna says.

"Bye Anna." Amie runs after Monica.

"Well everybody, I'm beat! Thanks for all your support." Anna bids her goodbyes.

Anna and Al head back to the dorm hand in hand.

"I'm so proud of you." Al says.

"Really? Thanks." Anna replys.

"No problem."

"Can you give me a massage? My neck and shoulders are so sore."

"I got you." When they get to Anna's room, Anna showers and then Al massages her neck and shoulders.

"You know, you never fail to amaze me." Anna says.

"Why is that?"

"What you said to my mom. You're a real sweetheart."

"You bring it out of me."

"Well, I'm glad." Anna smiles.

Friday evening rolls around and Anna, Al, and Will head to Anna's house.

"You're driving, Will." Anna peaks her head in Will's room. She is shocked to see Amber sitting on his bed.

"Okay. Gotcha." Will responds.

"Hey Amber." Anna says.

"Hey girl. Hope y'all have fun this weekend." Amber responds wishing she was invited.

"Try not to miss us too much." Anna says and heads to Al's room.

"Anna." Al says as Anna walks in.

"You ready, baby?" Anna asks.

"Yes. You sure it's alright for me to spend the night?"

"Yes. Will spends the night all the time. You two will sleep in the guest room. Just don't say anything about it until Granny leaves. She'll flip."

"Okay. Got it." Al grabs his and Anna's things and heads to Will's car.

"You are so wrong, Anna." Will chuckles as they all get in his car.

"What?" Anna asks confused.

"Try not to miss us too much this weekend? You hurt her feelings." Will responds.

"Ain't nobody got time for her sensitivity." Anna says.

"Be nice." Al whispers to Anna.

"You know it wasn't my intent to hurt that girls feelings."

"Whatever Anna. I know you better than that." Will responds.

"Well, she shouldn't have tried to make me feel bad for not inviting her."

"I guess." Will responds. When they pull up, Al gets a little nervous.

"You ready, Al?" Will asks.

"I don't know." Al responds.

"You already know mom. Granny is a little tough, but I know she'll like you." Anna responds. They get out of the car and head inside to the kitchen. Monica is finishing up dinner.

"Dinner smells wonderful." Al compliments as everyone takes a seat at the island.

"Thank you, Al." Monica responds.

"Hey y'all." Amie walks in. Everyone greets Amie. Suddenly, the doorbell rings.

"You ready?" Amie asks Al.

"No." He chuckles.

"I'll get it." Will runs to the door.

"Will! Hey there son!" Marie's face lights up.

"Come on in granny. I missed you." Will hugs Marie.

"How's school?" Marie asks Will.

"Couldn't be better. Aiming for straight A's."

"Great! Everyone in the kitchen?"

"Yes ma'am." Will follows Marie into the kitchen.

"Hey y'all." Marie exclaims scanning the room.

"Granny." Anna runs to Marie.

"Hey suga. I saw your game online. I know James is proud of you and so am I." Marie hugs and kisses Anna.

"Thanks so much!" Anna exclaims.

"G-Ma!" Amie hugs Marie.

"You look good, Amie. You still dancing?"

"Yes ma'am!" Amie sits back down.

"Hello Marie." Monica says still behind the stove.

"Monica." Marie says plainly.

"Uhm granny, I'd like for you to meet someone." Anna says avoiding the awkward moment between Marie and Monica.

"Who's this young man?" Marie asks

"This is Al. He plays with Will on the team and he's uhm the guy I'm currently talking to." Anna introduces.

"Talking to? Like a boyfriend?" Marie asks.

"Well, yes ma'am. I guess you could say that." Anna responds.

"Honey I'm old. Use terminology I know. Hello there son, what's your name again?" Marie looks Al up and down.

"I'm Alvin Peters, but everyone calls me Al."

"Nice to meet you, Alvin." They shake hands. There is an awkward silence as Marie stares at Al.

"Let's set the table." Anna says to Al, Will, and Amie. The four of them head to the dining room to prepare for dinner.

"That was awkward." Al says.

"You'll be fine. She always tries to intimidate guys we bring home." Anna responds.

"She did the same thing when she first met me, and now she loves me." Will adds.

"Just keep your cool and you'll be fine." Anna assures Al.

"I'll try." Al responds nervously.

"I promise everything will be okay." Anna kisses Al's cheek.

Once dinner is served everyone takes a seat at the table.

"One quick warning, Al. Granny has no filter. She says what's on her mind no matter who's around." Anna whispers to Al.

"With that being said, it may get really personal at this table." Amie adds. Marie takes her seat across from Anna and says grace. There is an awkward silence until Marie breaks it.

"So, Anna. How long have you been with Alvin?" Marie asks.

"I see you cut right to the chase. A couple months, ma'am." Anna smiles.

"I see. How'd you end up getting together?" Marie asks another question.

"Uhmm..." Anna gets nervous.

"Don't lie. You know I'll find out eventually." Marie stares at Anna.

"We started talking after a party, ma'am." Anna answers softly.

"I see. Are you still protecting your purity?" Marie asks disappointed.

"Granny...! Uhm yes ma'am." Anna lies.

"Hmm. What about you, Amie? Do you have a boyfriend?" Marie redirects her focus.

"No ma'am." Amie smiles.

"Good girl." Marie smiles back at Amie.

"Have you spoken with James?" Monica asks Marie.

"Why yes I have. I received my fourth letter yesterday. But, we'll talk about my son one on one. These children don't need to hear what I have to say."

"Whatever you say, Marie." Monica responds.

"So, when was the last time y'all went to church?" Marie asks.

"The last time we went was with you." Monica sighs.

"Well, why? That was a year ago." Marie asks angrily.

"We're busy. The kids have school and I have work."

"That's no excuse. You can give the Lord one day out of your oh so busy week. Sunday is the day you choose to rest."

"Even God rested." Amie giggles. Marie gives Amie her death stare.

"Y'all need to start going to church." Marie orders.

"We'll try, Marie." Monica responds.

"Don't lie. I'm just saying." Marie says. Nobody says anything after that.

Once they finish dinner, Marie and Monica talk in the living room as the kids clean and put the food away.

"She is tough." Al says.

"Here's the thing, she's not a fan of mom. So, we all get it when she's around." Anna responds.

In the living room, Marie is ready to give Monica a piece of her mind.

"James told me about your argument before he left. What's wrong with you? Don't you think that man deserves your support?" Marie asks.

"He talks too much. He has my support! That was just a rough day."

"A rough day? You really hurt him."

"I know. We already talked about it. We're fine now."

"Are you though? You can't just fix that type of damage in a letter. He sent me a letter crying out because you don't support him."

"What do you want from me Marie?? It's the same thing every time you come around. 'You don't support your husband. He needs your support.' I'm getting sick of it!"

"What's my problem?? You know I didn't support your marriage from the beginning. But, since you married anyways, you need to treat him right. You've always been ungrateful of his hard working."

"What??" Monica yells.

"That man breaks his back for you and how do you repay him?"

"I'm not going to sit here and let you degrade me. I'm a great wife. Nobody's perfect, Marie. Not even you! You probably drove your husband to his grave with your unrealistic high standards!"

"You leave my late husband out of this! We wouldn't be having this conversation if my son hadn't come to me for help."

"Whatever Marie. This conversation is over! I'm going upstairs. See yourself out when you're ready." Monica storms upstairs.

Marie goes to the dining room and takes a seat as Anna and Al finish clearing the table.

"Have a seat." Marie says to Anna and Al.

"What's up granny?" Anna asks.

"We need to talk. So, are y'all staying pure together?" Marie asks.

"Yes ma'am." Anna responds.

"Does Al know the high standard you girls live up to? A standard of pure living in every area of your lives. That means cuddling and sleeping in the same bed. You may see it as just cuddling, but it's the gateway for more to happen." Marie says.

"Yes ma'am." Anna responds.

"That goes for drinking and partying also. You're way too pretty and talented to be in that type of setting. You too Alvin. I've seen you play. Don't get caught up in partying and things of this world. All it'll do is leave you empty."

"Yes ma'am." Al says.

"Alright. I trust both of you to make wise decisions." Marie says as she heads to the kitchen.

"Hey granny." Will says to Marie.

"Let's play a couple games of spades so I can go. An old woman is getting tired." Marie smiles.

"You don't have to tell me twice." Will grabs the cards and sits at the dining room table with Marie and Amie. Anna and Al finish cleaning the kitchen. Marie keeps her eye on them the whole time.

"So, Will... tell me about this Alvin character." Marie says.

"That's my boy. Probably my best friend next to Anna."

"Really? So, he's a good guy? I trust your judgment."

"Trust me granny, if he wasn't cool for Anna, I never would've let them get together."

"Good. May I ask you a personal question? I know Anna tells you everything."

"Yes ma'am. Go ahead."

"Have they had sex?"

"No ma'am. Believe it or not, everything you say to Anna doesn't go in one ear and out the other. She's really adopted a lot of your morals."

"Glad to hear. Keep your eye on her for me. I only want what's best for her."

"I will and I know you do." They play one more game as Will tells Marie about Amber and Amie tells her about a boy she likes. When they finish, Marie gets ready to leave. She heads to the family room where Al and Anna are relaxing.

"I'm getting ready to head out." Marie says.

"Awh. Okay granny." Anna says.

"Listen here, Will put in a good word for you, Alvin. Continue to do right by my granddaughter."

"Yes ma'am." Al responds.

"I look forward to seeing more of the both of you." Marie says.

"Yes ma'am." Anna and Al respond.

"Tell your mother I said bye." Monica hugs everyone and leaves.

"You survived! She likes you!" Anna holds Al tight.

"Good look, Will." Al says.

"No problem. I like y'all together."

"Movie night?" Anna asks.

"Sounds good." Al responds.

"You're welcome to join if you'd like." Anna says to Amie. The four of them shower and get comfortable in the family room to watch movies.

The next morning, they wake up in the same spots they fell asleep in. Monica comes downstairs.

"Y'all want breakfast before you head out?"

"Yes!" They all respond.

"You alright, mom?" Anna asks.

"Yeah I am. You know how it is when she comes around. She means well. I understand why she's upset." Monica goes to cook breakfast.

"Their argument sounded really intense." Al says.

"That's normal." Anna laughs. They go wash up and relax in their pajamas until it's time to head back to campus that afternoon.

chapter four

December rolls around, and Anna's first basketball season has been going great. She has been averaging a triple-double as predicted and is a popular topic among college basketball fans. With only two losses on their record, Anna and her team have just won another home game. After the girls game ends Anna, Jenna, and Casey sit together to watch the boys play.

"So, Anna, aren't you glad you joined us this season?" Casey asks.

"Yes I am. I never thought playing for a team would be so much fun. All these years I've been sitting on my talent." Amber sits next to Anna as she finishes her statement.

"Hey y'all." Amber says.

"Hey." The girls respond.

"Great game, Anna." Amber says.

"Thanks." Anna replies as she directs her full attention to the game. Amber waits for Anna to tell her good game, but it never happens.

"So, I think I like Thomas, the center." Jenna says breaking the silence.

"I knew it!" Anna raises her voice.

"Can you put in a word for me, Anna?" Jenna asks

"Sure. I don't mind." Anna responds. The girls watch as Al assists the ball to Will, and he dunks it. They all go wild. Everyone stands but Amber. Will looks over to Anna and mouths "that was for you."

"That's my best friend!" Anna yells. After that, Amber gets angry.

"You alright over there, Amber?" Casey asks.

"No, I'm not, actually. Why'd he dedicate that to Anna and not me?" Amber asks angrily.

"Uhm, because I told him to dedicate his next dunk to his best friend. Number two, you never sit here, so he probably doesn't even know you're over here. I'ma need you to get out of your little feelings." Anna says with an attitude. Amber just gets up and walks away.

"What's wrong with her?" Jenna asks.

"Who knows? She's always in her feelings for no reason." Casey responds.

Once the game ends, Anna and the girls make their way to the court to wait for the guys. Thomas is the first to come out.

"Great game Thomas!" Anna says.

"Thanks! Same to you! You've become a hot commodity. Last night my dad called and asked if I knew you."

"Really? Wow."

"Yeah. Keep it up!"

"Before you go, have you met Jenna?"

"Nope. She's the only girl on the team I don't know."

"Hey Jenna!" Anna calls out.

"What's up Anna?" Jenna walks over.

"Thomas, this is Jenna. Jenna, this is Thomas."

"Nice to meet you." Thomas says. Seconds later, Al comes out of the locker room.

"Welp, there goes Al. You two have fun." Anna walks over to Al.

"Hey babe." Al kisses Anna.

"Great game baby. I see you tryina hoop like me." Anna laughs.

"Funny. You ready?"

"Yeah. Let me speak to Will real quick." Anna runs over to Will before he can get to Amber.

"Anna! Did you see the shout out?" Will asks.

"You know I did! Great game, bestie."

"Thanks. Good game to you also."

"Thanks, but you'd better get to your girl. She's mad."

"About what? What'd you do??"

"It's what you did." Anna runs to Al before Will can respond. She watches as Amber confronts Will about the shout out.

Anna and Al get in his truck and leave the gym.

"Where are we going?" Anna asks, noticing Al isn't driving in the direction of the dorms.

"Quick detour." They pull up to a garden on campus with tables and benches spread around. People come here to chill and study when the weather permits.

"What are we doing here?" Anna asks.

"Just get out." Al says as he opens his door.

"Uhm... it's 35 degrees outside."

"Just do it." Al says. Anna rolls her eyes and gets out of the car. She follows Al into the garden.

"It's cold, Alvin." Anna calls Al by his full first name when she's angry.

"Just bear with me for a few more minutes."

"Fine." Anna rolls her eyes again.

"Well, Anna Marie Winefield, we've been dating for three months now. And I must say I have enjoyed every minute of it. With that being said, I want to present you with this." Al hands Anna a small jewelry box.

"What's this?" Anna asks.

"Open it." Al responds. Anna opens the box, and inside is a ring.

"Wh-what's this for? It's beautiful."

"Well Anna... I've been wanting to do this for some time, but I wanted to wait until the perfect moment. I want to make things official. I... want you to be my girlfriend. The ring is a promise ring. Just a symbol of how deep my feelings are for you."

"Wow."

"So... what do you say?"

"Yes! I'd love to be your girlfriend!" Anna puts the ring on and hugs Al tight.

"You are absolutely amazing, Anna."

"So are you!" Anna responds with a huge smile on her face.

"Now let's get you out of the cold." Al grabs Anna's hand as they head back to the dorms.

When they get to the dorm, Anna is summoned to Will's room.

"What's up Will?" Anna asks

"What's your problem with Amber?" Will asks angrily.

"Where's this coming from?"

"She told me you always have an attitude with her."

"What?? Only after she comes at me sideways!"

"I know you're not the biggest fan of girls, but can you give her a chance?"

"Look Will, I don't trust her."

"Why?? She hasn't done anything to you!" Will raises his voice.

"Here's the problem I have... after y'all brought those girls back to y'alls rooms after the last party, she asked me questions to check up on you. I don't like that. If she wants to know who you're bringing to the room, she needs to ask you. That was messy of her. You know from experience that I don't like that."

"Why didn't you just tell me that?"

"Because I wanted to give her a chance. But, if she keeps coming at me sideways, I'm gonna have to shut it down quick fast and in a hurry."

"You are a piece of work, Anna. But, thanks for having my back. I'll talk to her."

"We been best friends since middle school. I'll always have your back." Anna high fives Will and he notices the ring.

"I see you said yes."

"To Al? Yes I did."

"So, you really like him?"

"Yeah, I really do."

"I'm happy for y'all. Hopefully one day you'll feel the same about Amber and me."

"I want to... she just has to give me a reason to."

"I'm glad you're open to it." They hug and Anna heads to her room.

Time passes, and both Al and Anna continue to put in work on the basketball court. Both the men's and the women's teams end up in their league finals. Once the season ends, everyone focuses in on school. Finals come around and finally the semester is coming to a close.

"We made it!" Anna says to Al, Will, and Amber as they lounge in a common area.

"Yes we did! We're all gonna be juniors next year!" Amber adds.

"And Anna survived her first year of playing ball." Will says.

"I'm proud of you." Al says to Anna.

"Thanks, baby." Anna responds.

"I'm starving." Amber says.

"Me too." Will adds.

"How about Will and I go pick something up real quick?" Al offers.

"Sounds good." Will replies.

"I wanna go." Anna says.

"Guys only. Y'all want pizza?" Will asks.

"That's fine." Anna rolls her eyes. The guys go to get the food as Anna and Amber sit in silence.

"You know they did that on purpose, right?" Anna shakes her head.

"Yeah." Amber sighs.

"Look Amber... I'll be honest and say I didn't like you for Will. Not because you're not a nice girl, but I just didn't trust you. You did some messy things and my guard went up."

"I see... and I didn't trust you because you and Will are so close. I was afraid that y'all were secretly in love."

"In love... with Will? Hahahaha! He's literally like a brother. Been in my life since we were in middle school. We've never had any feelings for each other."

"And the only reason I questioned you about him was because of my own insecurities. I meant no harm."

"I say we call a truce. Let's forget any problems we've had with each other and move forward in this friendship."

"I agree." Amber smiles as they shake hands. When the guys get back, they are happy to see Anna and Amber talking and getting along.

The weekend comes around and Anna goes home. When she gets there, Amie and Monica are watching television.

"Hey y'all." Anna says.

"Hey baby." Monica responds.

"Hey Anna." Amie says back.

"Have you talked to your father?" Monica asks Anna.

"Yeah. Just wrote him back yesterday." Anna responds.

"So, he told you he'll be back in a month?" Monica asks.

"Yes ma'am. He did."

"I was thinking we could throw him a surprise party. Just invite Marie and our closest friends. You can bring Will and Al."

"Sounds like a good idea. Dad loves surprises." Anna adds. That day, they begin the party arrangements.

After a month of planning, the day of James' arrival is here. All of the family's closest friends are at the house along with Marie. Al, Will, Amber, and Amie are with Anna in her room.

"Anna, breathe." Al says.

"I'm just so nervous and excited at the same time." Anna explains.

"Me too." Amie concurs.

"I'm really excited to finally meet him forreal." Al says.

"He's gonna love you." Anna winks at Al. Once Anna is ready, they all head downstairs.

"You ready? They should be here soon." Monica smiles.

"This was a great idea, Monica. Good job coordinating things." Marie compliments Monica.

"Thanks, but I couldn't have done it without you." Monica responds surprised. Suddenly, there is a ring at the doorbell.

"Everyone hide!" Monica says as her heart begins to pound hard. Everyone except Anna, Amie, Monica, and Marie hide. Monica goes to the door and opens it. To her surprise, there are two men in uniform standing there. Monica's first reaction is panic.

"What's going on officers?" Monica begins shaking as a few tears form in her eyes.

"Mrs. Winefield... uhm..." One of the officers begins.

"What's going on??" Monica asks angrily.

"A few hours ago, we learned that as James was heading to the airport, a malfunction happened with the helicopter. The pilot could not gain control of the helicopter, and it crashed." One of the officers says.

"But... they're alright." Monica tries to assure herself.

"No ma'am. All who were in the helicopter were killed." The other officer adds. Everyone is speechless.

"Thank you, officers." Monica says still shaking. The officers salute Monica, and leave. Monica closes the door with tears in her eyes.

"So, you're telling me my dad is dead??" Anna asks as everyone comes out of their hiding spots. Monica has no words. Anna falls into Al's arms crying hysterically and Amie runs to her room. Tears slide down Will's face as he goes to comfort Monica. She falls to her knees and Will just holds her.

"Uhm... I'm going to have to ask everyone except immediate family to leave. Thank you all for coming, but the party's over. Anna's friends, you're fine. But everyone else, we'll be in touch with the funeral arrangements." Marie says. Everyone leaves and Marie walks to the family room to cry privately.

Anna runs upstairs to her room and Al follows. Anna sits on her bed as Al just stands at the door not knowing what to say.

"This can't be real. Maybe I'm dreaming. I refuse to believe my dad is gone forever. Tell me he's not gone, Al!" Anna begins to cry again. Al sits on the bed and pulls Anna close. He rubs his fingers through her hair as she cries. Downstairs, Will walks Monica to the family room. Nobody says anything. They just let the tears flow. Will then goes upstairs to see about Amie.

"You alright, Amie?" Will asks.

"No! My daddy's dead! Why did he have to go?? He's supposed to be here now enjoying his surprise!"

"I'm so sorry, Amie." Will attempts to comfort her. Amie says nothing. Will goes to the hall and sits on the floor against the wall.

"Why God??" Will asks as he begins to cry.

After a couple hours of silence, everyone is all cried out. Anna looks up at Al.

"Thanks for being here." Anna says as a couple more tears slide down her face.

"I'll always be here for you." They kiss and Al wipes Anna's face.

"Let's go downstairs." Anna says. When they get to the kitchen, everyone is sitting down as Marie makes tea.

"Thanks for the words of encouragement, Marie." Monica says.

"You're so strong, granny." Anna says.

"My faith in God is what keeps me, honey. I know this is hard news to take in. Grieve as long as you need to, but know your father's death was not in vain. Your father is a hero. We're going to see him again. To be absent from the body is to be present with the Lord."

"I love you, granny." Anna confides as the phone rings and Monica goes to answer it.

"I love you too, baby. Be encouraged. You'll make it through this." Marie hugs Anna.

"What's wrong, mom?" Anna asks as Monica walks back into the kitchen looking distressed.

"Uhm... Jim Kelly was in the helicopter. That was his wife." Monica says.

"Awh man." Anna says as a few more tears fall.

"I'll uhm... call you tomorrow." Monica says as Marie prepares to leave.

"Okay. Love y'all." Marie lets herself out.

"So, what now, mom?" Anna asks.

"We pick up the pieces and move forward. As hard as it may be, we have no choice. We'll get through this." Monica responds.

"I hope so." Anna says.

"Well, I'm gonna head to bed. Got a long day of planning tomorrow." Monica hugs everyone and heads upstairs.

"I say we should all call it a night." Anna says.

"Yeah, we should." Will concurs. He and Amber head to the guest room and Anna and Al head to her room. Will gives Amber the bed, and he sleeps on the floor.

"You want me on the floor?" Al asks Anna.

"No. I need to be close to you tonight." Anna responds.

"You sure?"

"Yes. I feel like everything's going to be okay when I'm in your arms." Anna confides. They shower and get in bed. Al holds Anna as she cries herself to sleep.

The next morning, Anna wakes up early. As she waits on Al to wake up, she watches the DVD James made for her while overseas and then she watches their last one-on-one game.

"What's this?" Al asks as he wakes up.

"The last game I played with my dad."

"He's pretty good." Al says.

"Pretty good? My dad's the best. He's the reason I can bust your butt on the court now. He almost went pro after college." Anna smiles hard.

"There she is." Al smiles.

"Who?"

"That beautiful smile of yours. Whenever you start to feel sad, I dare you to think of a happy memory with him and watch it make you smile. That's what I did when my dad died. Worked every time."

"I'll try to do that. It feels good to smile."

"I know from firsthand experience that it feels like you won't get through this, but you will."

"I really appreciate you being here for me." Anna says.

"Get used to it because I'm here for the long run." Al assures Anna. They get up and get dressed. When they get downstairs, Amber and Will are waiting on them.

"Ready?" Anna asks them.

"Yeah." They both respond. Anna goes to Monica's room.

"Yeah." They both respond. Anna goes to Monica's room.

"Mom, how you holding up?" Anna asks.

"I'll be fine. You alright?" Monica asks.

"Yes ma'am. We're about to head out. Let me know all the details."

"I will. Take it easy. Don't overwork yourself or separate yourself from everyone. I know how you are. Let people be there for you. Maybe you should sit out on a couple practices."

"Now's not the time to stop my passion. That's my therapy."

"Just take it easy."

"I will. Love you." Anna hugs her mother.

"Love you too. Be safe." Monica adds. Anna goes downstairs and they head back to campus. School is out, but summer conditioning is in session.

A week and a half later, the funeral takes place. Anna, Will, and Al ride in the limo with Monica, Marie, and Amie. Once the limo arrives at the church, they slowly make their way to the front of the sanctuary and sit in their seats. The entire ceremony is beautiful and uplifting. People all over the building are in tears as Marie finds the strength to sing a song to her son. When the service comes to a close, everyone heads to the gravesite to say their last goodbyes to James. Marie's pastor says a few words, prays, and ends the service. The immediate family stays around to watch the burial of James' casket.

"The service was beautiful." Marie says once the burial process is over.

"Yes it was." Monica agrees.

"I just can't believe he's gone." Anna says. Marie hugs Anna.

"I know it's hard. If you ever need a getaway, you're free to come over anytime. You too Amie." Marie says.

"Yes ma'am." Anna and Amie respond.

"You all hungry?" Monica asks.

"Yes!" Amie exclaims.

"No. I just wanna go back to campus." Anna responds.

"Alright. Keep an eye on her for me." Monica says quietly to Will and Al. Monica, Marie, and Amie go out to eat.

"You alright Anna?" Al asks. She doesn't respond and starts walking to Will's car.

"Something you should know about Anna is that she shuts down when she's depressed. You just have to be patient with her. Don't be surprised if she pulls away. Give her time, and she'll be fine." Will says to Al.

"Thanks for the heads up." Al says at the walk to Will's car. When they get to campus, Anna goes straight to her room slamming the door behind her. Al tries to open it, but it's locked. Will feels bad as he stands in his doorway watching Al walk to his room with his head down.

chapter five

A month passes and Anna is still struggling with her father's death. She is not fully engaged into basketball practice of her summer classes. She hasn't even been hanging with Al or the guys. After class and practice, Anna locks herself in her room. Even her eating habits have changed to the point that she is losing weight as an unhealthy rate. One afternoon, Anna is in her room watching the DVD of her game with James. She's been faithfully watching it every day. Suddenly, there is a knock at the door.

"Hey guys. Come in." Anna says to Jenna and Casey.

"Whoa! I've never seen your room this clean." Jenna laughs.

"All I do is clean. What's up?"

"How are you, girl? You've been in this room for a month." Casey says.

"I go to class and practice."

"But, you're not there mentally." Casey says.

"And you leave as soon as practice lets out." Jenna adds.

"We've come to kidnap you. You need to get out of here." Casey says.

"And you need to eat. You've gotten so skinny!" Jenna adds.

"I don't wanna go anywhere."

"Nope! Get dressed and let's go!" Casey demands.

"But-"

"No buts. Let's go." Jenna says.

"Fine." Anna rolls her eyes.

Once Anna is dressed and has her hair done, the girls go to the cafeteria. As soon as they find a table, Anna sees Al sitting by himself. Suddenly, a girl approaches him, hugs him, and sits at his table.

"Uhm, who's that?" Anna raises her left eyebrow.

"That's Sarah." Jenna responds.

"What's she doing with my boyfriend?"

"I don't know. They've been together a lot lately. But, can you really be upset? You've been ignoring him for a month." Jenna says. Anna gets up and walks to Al and Sarah's table.

"Anna..." Al says when he sees her.

"Who's this, Al?" Anna raises her voice.

"Can you lower your voice, please? This is Sarah." Al answers.

"I know her name, but what are you doing together?" Anna asks with an attitude.

"I'm uhm... gonna go." Sarah says.

"Yeah go!" Anna says as Sarah walks away.

"What's wrong with you?" Al asks.

"While I'm struggling with the death of my dad, you're out here with other women!"

"Hold up! So, you can have a guy best friend, but I can't hang out with a girl friend?? That's not how the world works, Anna! You haven't talked to me in a month! I know you're going through a tough situation, but at least let me be there for you! If you don't stop and realize the world doesn't revolve around you, we're not gonna work."

"What?"

"My feelings are hurt, Anna. The girl I love won't let me into her heart. You've put up a wall that I can't break through. Until you move past your father's death, I think we should take a break."

"You're kidding, right?"

"What do you expect from me, Anna? I've called and text you every day for the past month and you continue to ignore me. I know it's hard to lose a parent. I've been through it... I gotta go. Call me when you're ready to move forward." Al walks away.

"What just happened?" Casey and Jenna run to Anna.

"He just broke up with me. I can't believe him!"

"I'm sorry baby girl. But-"Casey begins.

"But what?? Don't take his side! Y'all need to stay away from me." Anna runs to her room.

That night, Will tries to talk to Anna. He knocks and she lets him in.

"Hey Will." Anna says.

"I've seen you depressed before, but never like this. You're pushing everyone away. I know you miss dad, but he's gone. The quicker you come to terms with that, the easier it will be to move on."

"But-"

"But nothing, Anna. I think you should see a therapist. That might help you move through the grieving process."

"I'm not going to see a therapist. What I look like?"

"Someone that needs help. Sarah and Al told me what happened today. That's so out of character for you. I'm disappointed, Anna. When was the last time you talked to Amie or mom? Open your eyes, Anna. I hope you snap back into reality before you look around and everyone around you has moved on." Will leaves Anna's room.

A week later, Anna decides to make a trip home. When she gets in the house, Monica and Amie are in the kitchen talking.

"Well hello there." Monica says shocked to see Anna.

"Sorry I haven't been around. I've really been struggling to move forward."

"I understand, but-"Monica begins.

"But what? My dad, your husband is dead. Am I the only one still hurting?"

"Of course not, Anna. We're all hurting. But, you have to move forward. He's gone, Anna. Will called last night. What's going on with you?" Monica asks.

"I just really miss him. That's all."

"So shut everybody off?"

"I didn't come here for this." Anna says walking to the door.

"Anna, wait!" Monica calls out. Anna leaves tearing up. She gets in her car and drives to Marie's house. As Anna pulls up to Marie's house, Marie is outside gardening. Anna quickly gets out of her car and approaches Marie.

"Anna! What a surprise!" Marie smiles.

"Granny! I need you!" Anna begins to cry.

"Oh baby! What's wrong?"

"I still can't believe he's gone!"

"Awh, come here, baby." Marie welcomes a hug and Anna falls into her arms. Marie walks Anna into the house.

"Why'd he have to go?" Anna asks still crying. Marie sits on the couch with Anna and comforts her until she calms down.

"I don't have an answer for you. Death is a part of life. No one knows when it's their time to go."

"But, why did he have to go so early? I didn't get to say goodbye!" Anna tears up again.

"I know it's hard. I think about him every day. Yeah, I become sad, but I remember he didn't die in vain."

"How are you so strong?"

"My relationship with God is what's kept me. With Him, I have a comfort and a peace that passes all understanding."

"I need that."

"It's a free gift. All you have to do is ask Him for it. You should come to church with me this Sunday."

"Can I stay here until then? I need a break from everything."

"You can stay as long as you'd like. You hungry? Dinner's in the oven."

"No ma'am. I'm not."

"Well, you need to eat. You've lost a lot of weight."

"I haven't had much of an appetite the past month."

"Oh baby, we're gonna get you through this. Get settled and I'm gonna finish gardening. You're free to anything in here."

"Thanks granny. I love you."

"I love you too, baby." Marie goes outside as Anna goes to the guest room and gets comfortable.

An hour later, Marie walks into Anna's room.

"You okay in here?" Marie asks.

"Yes ma'am."

"Come on. Dinner's ready." Marie leaves the room. Anna washes her hands and goes into the kitchen. She and Marie sit down to enjoy dinner.

"This is bomb." Anna says.

"Thank you. So, how's that boy?"

"Who? Al?"

"Yes, him."

"I don't know. I guess he's good. We're not together anymore."

"Why not?"

"He's upset with me. I've been avoiding him since the funeral. To be honest, I've been avoiding all my friends and teammates."

"That's not good. You need people around you... especially when you're grieving."

"I just haven't wanted to be bothered."

"We're gonna nurse you back to complete mental and physical health this week. You'll be back to normal by Sunday."

"You sound so confident."

"I am. But, you have to be open to the process."

"I'm open. I don't like feeling like this all the time."

"I understand. You'll be fine. One day, you'll look back on this week and be grateful you made this decision."

"I hope so." Anna responds. After dinner, Anna and Marie clean the kitchen. Soon after, the two go to bed. Not wanting to be alone, Anna sleeps with Marie.

After spending a week with Marie, Anna heads home on Sunday afternoon. She walks into the house to find Monica cooking dinner.

"Hey mom." Anna says standing in the kitchen doorway.

"Anna." Monica says not looking up. There is a long pause.

"Look, I'm sorry for storming out the other day. My attitude was out of line." Anna says.

"Yes it was. You know I don't tolerate disrespect."

"I know. But, I'm good now. I spent the week with granny, and she helped me through my depression."

"That's good. Sit down and tell me about it." Monica says. Anna takes a seat at the island as Amie walks in.

"What are you doing here?" Amie asks Anna.

"Sit down and listen." Monica orders Amie. Amie sits next to Anna.

"Well, I stayed with granny all week. She made me promise to submit to the process of moving forward. Basically, every morning, we woke up early to do a devotion and pray." Anna begins.

"You praying?" Amie laughs.

"Shut up chump. Anyways, we went to bible study Wednesday night and I swear the pastor was speaking directly to me. And then today, we went to church. Yet again, the message was just what I needed to hear. I went forward for the altar call, and pastor prayed for me. I've never felt so free. I feel a peace and contentment I've never felt." Anna smiles.

"That's good. I'm glad." Monica says.

"It's about time." Amie says.

"What?" Anna asks.

"Granny made us do the same thing a month ago." Amie says.

"How'd I miss it?" Anna asks a little angry.

"You miss out when you pull away from the ones closest to you." Monica says.

"Anna sits in silence for a few minutes.

"I'll be back!" Anna says as she grabs her keys and runs to her car knowing Will is home. When she pulls up to his house, she runs to the door and knocks. Will's grandmother answers the door.

"Anna..." Will's grandmother says confused.

"Hi G-Ma. Is Will here?"

"Yes he is. Come in." The woman says. She calls out Will's name as Anna sits in the living room. Will comes down the stairs and is surprised to see Anna.

"Anna... hey." Will says.

"Hey Will."

"What's going on? I'm surprised to see you of all people."

"I'm so sorry for how I've been acting! I spent the last week with granny and she helped me through my problems. I've been a complete jerk to you and everyone else. Please say you forgive me."

"You know I do. I've been waiting for you to come to your senses."

"So, you're telling me I have my best friend back?"

"I never left." Will says as Anna runs into his arms.

"I missed you so much! Come over for dinner."

"I'm there. I'm so sick of this house. Too many rules." Will laughs as he goes to pack an overnight bag.

Dinner is ready when Anna and Will get to the house. Anna, Will, Monica, and Amie sit at the table to eat.

"It feels so good to have my appetite back." Anna says.

"Thank God. You've gotten so skinny." Amie says.

"I missed coming around." Will says.

"Awh, we missed you too, Will. Anna, what happened to those two girls from the team?" Monica inquires.

"Jenna and Casey? I need to call them tomorrow. I own them an apology." Anna answers.

"Why?" Amie asks.

"I went off on them because they took Al's side over something stupid."

"What's going on with Al?" Monica asks.

"He broke up with me." Anna answers.

"That jerk!" Amie raises her voice.

"No, it was my fault. I've been avoiding him since the funeral." Anna says looking at the ring he gave her.

"I see you still wear the promise ring." Monica says.

"Yeah. I love him. I was so stupid for shutting him out." Anna says.

"It'll all work out." Monica says.

"After dinner, Will and Anna go to Anna's room and lay in Anna's bed.

"Will, who's that Sarah girl?" Anna asks Will.

"She'll be a sophomore in the fall. She's a cheerleader. Damen introduced us to her. She's just cool people."

'There's nothing going on between her and Al?"

"Not that I know of. She's actually been wanting to meet you for a while."

"She must think I'm a complete jerk."

"Yeah. The way you acted up."

"You know I'm overprotective. How's Amber?"

"She's good. We have a date planned as soon as we get back to school."

"You miss her, huh?"

"Yeah I do."

"Do you love her?"

"I don't know about love, but I do like her a lot."

"I'm happy for you. I like seeing you like this opposed to being a man-whore."

"I like it too." Will smiles.

"I hope Al and I make it through this." A tear rolls down Anna's face.

"Come here." Will says. Anna slides over and lays her head on Will's chest.

"I don't know what to do." Anna says.

"Now, Al's my boy and all, but he's one dumb cat if he lets you go. I'll never let him hear the end of it."

"Really?" Anna smiles.

"Yes. I don't just call you my best friend for no reason. We've been cool since we were kids. You come before any guy on the team." Will says as he gives Anna a wet willie.

"Ew! Jerk!" Anna laughs. The two of them laugh and lay in bed until they fall asleep.

The next morning, Anna and Will wake up and go outside to play ball.

"You need to call Casey and Jenna." Will says after they finish a game.

"I don't know what to say."

"Start by apologizing. Invite them over." Will says. Anna goes inside to call them. A few minutes later, she comes back outside.

"They're on their way." Anna says.

"Ready for another game?" Will asks.

"Let's go!" Anna yells. As they play a second game, Jenna and Casey pull up. They get out and watch Anna and Will finish the game.

"Hey guys." Anna says once they finish up.

"Hey." Jenna says.

"What was so urgent?" Casey asks impatiently.

"I wanna apologize for how I acted last week. Y'all were just trying to help, and I was a jerk." Anna says.

"Yeah, you were. But, it's cool. You're forgiven." Casey says smiling.

"Awh! Group hug!" Anna yells as the three of them hug.

"Y'all ain't tryina go two on two, though." Will says.

"Let's go! We're always ready to play!" Casey says.

"Y'all against me and Anna." Will suggests.

"Let's get it." Jenna laughs. The girls suit up and the two teams go to war on the court. After a close game, Will and Anna pull off the win.

"Undefeated!" Anna yells.

"Really?" Jenna asks.

"We've never lost a game together." Will smiles at Anna.

"Sweet." Jenna says.

"Y'all wanna come in and chill?" Anna asks.

"Sounds good." Casey responds. The four of them go inside and watch TV for a while. After watching TV, the gang gets hungry.

"Y'all hungry?" Anna asks.

"Yes!" Everyone exclaims.

"I'm gonna cook breakfast. You can come in the kitchen if you want." Anna offers. She gets up and everyone follows. Jenna, Casey, and Will sit at the island as Anna begins cooking.

"So, what are you gonna do about Al?" Casey asks.

"I don't know. I haven't thought much about it." Anna responds.

"Stop lyin'!" Will stares at Anna.

"Okay, fine. I think about it all the time. I'm just gonna tell him what was going on with me. Apologize and ask him to take me back." Anna says.

"What if that doesn't work?" Jenna asks.

"Oh, it's gonna work." Anna responds angrily.

"Sorry, you're right. Y'all were perfect for each other." Jenna responds apologetically.

"Yeah. We were. Anna smiles.

"Ready for school in a month?" Casey asks.

"Nope!" Will answers.

"Me either." Jenna responds.

"I'm ready to dominate on the court, though." Will pretends to shoot a basketball.

"I'm ready to bust all of y'all in one on one before the season starts." Anna says.

"I don't know, Anna. Ya boy Joey's been practicing. Al's been in the gym hard, too." Will says.

"Please! I'll take both of them one on one right now."

"We'll see." Will laughs.

"I wanna plan something big when we get back. Like, a big dinner or something." Anna says.

"You always tryina eat." Will laughs.

"You right. I love food!" Anna smiles.

"That's why we're best friends." Will smiles at Anna.

"So, are you guys down? We can all dress up and enjoy dinner." Anna says.

"You dressing up for fun? This I have to see! Let's do it." Will says to Anna.

"Great! Texting everybody right now." Anna picks up her phone. Once the food is ready, everyone eats.

"That was amazing, Anna!" Casey says.

"Thanks. My dad used to make this for me every Saturday. His own special pancake recipe." Anna smiles.

"I'm so glad you've come to terms with everything. I miss that smile." Will says.

"I'm really happier than I've been in a long time. Thanks for being here for me. I really appreciate it." Anna says.

"Awh. Group hug." Casey says as they all hug. After cleaning up, Jenna and Casey head home. Will and Anna go lounge in front of the TV.

"It feels good to relax!" Anna says.

"Don't get too used to it. It all ends in a month." Will says as the two of them laugh.

chapter six

A month passes and it's finally time to start up a new school year. Will and Anna pack and head to school together.

"You ready for this?" Will asks.

"No." Anna responds.

"Don't worry. Everything will be fine chump." Will assures Anna.

"Thanks. If things don't go right, I'm sleeping in your room tonight." Anna says.

"About that... Amber might be here." Will says.

"Ew. Never mind." Anna laughs as they pull up to the school. The two of them go check in and head to the dorm. When they get there, Joey is in the hallway.

"My boy Joey!" Will yells.

"What up Will! Anna!" Joey high fives Will and Anna jumps in his arms.

"I missed ya!" Anna says.

"I missed you too. I been practicing. Ready to get beat?" Joey asks.

"Haha. Never. But, I'm ready whenever you are." Anna laughs.

Anna and Will take their things to their rooms. Once Anna finishes, she goes to Will's room.

"Have you seen Al?" Anna asks.

"Yeah. He just came by. He's in his room."

"That negro came here, but didn't stop to see me?" Anna asks angrily.

"Just go see him." Will responds. Anna doesn't say anything; she just walks down the hall to Al's room. She knocks three times and waits. A couple seconds later, Al opens the door.

"Anna... hi." Al says shocked.

"Hey. May I come in?" Anna asks timidly.

"Uh, yeah." Al looks around the hall and lets her in.

"So, how was your summer?" Anna asks.

"It was cool. Didn't do too much. Yours?"

"The same... look, I wanted to apologize. I experience another level of depression, and I didn't know how to handle it. So, I pushed you away. But, I spent some time with my granny, and she helped me through it."

"That's good. It's cool."

"It's cool? That's all you have to say?" Anna asks.

"I'm glad you're good now. What do you expect me to say?"

"How about 'awh baby, I missed you.' I'm pouring my heart out to you, and you say it's cool?"

"Look Anna, I accepted your apology. We haven't talked in months. You don't just expect things to go back to how they were, do you?"

"Yes! Yes I do! What we had was real. You can't just give up on us."

"You hurt me, Anna. I've never been the relationship type. But, I gave you a chance, and look at us now... that scene you pulled in the caf... I think we could be friends... but that's it." Al says.

"You're kidding me, right? Beginning of the school year prank? It has to be."

"I'm serious, Anna. This is not a prank."

"So, what about that night at the park? When you asked me to be your girl? What happened to being here for the long run?"

"Things and people change, Anna. Look, I've been talking to someone else over the past couple of weeks."

"What?? Who is it? Sarah?"

"Yes, as a matter of fact, it is her."

"I knew it!"

"Nothing was going on between us when that incident in the caf happened. She reached out to me like two weeks ago. We've been talking every day since."

"I can't believe you. So, everything you said to me was a lie? It had to have been since you moved on so fast."

"No, Anna. I really liked you."

"Liked... wow! I'm in love with you, Al. But, I guess it doesn't matter anymore. Have a nice life. Here." Anna takes off the promise ring and hands it to Al. Al is shocked.

"Anna... we can still be cool."

"I'm good. Bye, Al." Anna turns and begins to tear up. She opens the door and sees Sarah about to knock.

"Anna? Hi." Sarah smiles.

"He's all yours." Anna says and walks down the hall.

"What was that about?" Sarah asks.

"Nothing." Al responds as he looks at the ring and puts it in his pocket.

"Ready?"

"Yeah. Let me finish getting dressed." Al responds. Anna runs to Will's room wiping her eyes.

"How'd it go?" Will asks.

"Horrible! We're done for good. He's dating Sarah." Anna breaks out in a full cry.

"Since when?" Will asks.

"Two weeks ago." Anna barely gets out. Will hugs Anna to comfort her. Suddenly, there is a knock at the door. Anna lies on the bed crying as Will answers it.

"Hey baby!" Amber says. Will grabs her and hugs her tight.

"I missed you girl!" Will responds.

"Me too." Amber kisses him. Al and Sarah begin to walk down the hall.

"Can you go inside? Talk to Anna. She needs a girls' advice." Will says. Amber walks inside closing the door.

"Hey Will." Sarah says as they pass him.

"Hey Sarah. Al, can I talk to you for a minute?" Will asks.

"Sure." Al responds. Sarah stops at the main door as Al runs to Will.

"Really dude?" Will asks quietly.

"You saw firsthand how Anna treated me."

"But, you pay her back by dating another girl two weeks later? That's not cool."

"We've not even together. We've really just been hanging out."

"Whatever man. I'm disappointed. This isn't cool at all."

"So, we're not cool either?" Al asks.

"No, we are. But, I want nothing to do with you and Sarah. If she's there, I won't be. Anna will get mad at me if I stop kickin' it with you, so leave before I really get upset about you hurting her." Will and Al dap as Al leaves.

Will walks into the room and Amber is on the bed comforting Anna.

"You good, Anna?" Will asks.

"I'll be fine. What'd you and Al talk about?" Anna asks.

"I told him what he did isn't cool."

"Y'all are still cool, right?" Anna asks.

"Yeah. I know you too well." Will smiles.

"Huh?" Amber asks confused.

"I don't let Will stop being friends with mutual friends if we break up. They were cool before we got together, so I don't want my drama to mess up a great relationship." Anna answers.

"You really are of a different breed." Amber says.

"It comes with the territory of having all guy friends." Anna smiles.

"I guess." Amber laughs.

"Well, I'm gonna go. Y'all enjoy your day together." Anna gets up.

"You don't have to go, Anna." Amber says.

"Y'all haven't seen each other in a while. I'll dump my problems on you another time. I need to be alone, anyways."

"Fine. Call me if you need anything." Will hugs Anna.

"You know I won't. I'll bother Joey if I need anything." Anna smiles and goes to her room. Trying not to cry again, she bumps music and unpacks. Once she finishes, she lies down for a nap.

When Anna wakes up, Joey is staring at her with a goofy look.

"What the hell, Joey?" Anna asks.

"I've been assigned to you for the rest of the day." Joey smiles.

"I hate Will."

"Today is forget Al day. That's my dawg, but he's dumb for his decision."

"I'm glad you think so. So, since I know you're not going to leave me alone, what are we doing tonight?"

"We're going to the movies with some of the guys. Then, we're going to eat."

"Yay food! I'm down."

"All of your expenses will be taken care of by yours truly."

"So, all I had to do was get my heart broken for free food?" Anna laughs.

"Very funny. Get dressed so we can head out." Joey laughs as he leaves. Once Anna is dressed, she heads out with Joey and five other teammates. After a fun night, they head to campus and prepare for classes the next day.

Anna wakes up and doesn't want to go to class when she realizes half of her classes are with Al.

"You ready?" Will walks into Anna's room.

"No! Al is in like half of my classes." Anna responds.

"Oh lord. Well, let's go so you don't have to sit next to him." Will suggests. They get to class and pick their seats. Joey walks in next and site on the opposite side of Anna. When Al gets there, he sits on the row behind Anna with a few other teammates.

"Last night was fun." Thomas says.

"Yeah it was!" Anna turns around and high fives Thomas, who is sitting next to Al.

"What'd y'all do?" Al asks jealous.

"Dinner and a movie." Joey responds.

"No invite?" Al asks a little hurt.

"No couples allowed. Will wasn't there." Thomas responds. Anna laughs to herself as Al sits there in silence.

"You ready to get dunked on again, Joey?" Anna asks.

"Funny. I been practicing hard this summer." Joey responds.

"We'll see. Rematch Friday? Give you some time to prepare?" Anna laughs.

"Let's do it." Joey says.

"Then, I'm taking on the winner." Will says.

"So, you wanna get dunked on too?" Anna asks.

"You know better." Will says as they all laugh.

"Haha. I missed you guys!" Anna smiles as the professor walks in.

As Anna gets back into the swing of school, she is making it fine without Al. Friday rolls around, and it's time for her game with Joey. The whole guys' team shows up along with a few girls from the women's team.

"This is real." Anna says into the stands.

"You got it." Jenna responds.

"Oh trust. I'm not worried." Anna assures herself.

"You should be." Joey walks past her. As Anna and Joey warm up on opposite sides of the court, Anna freezes as Al walks in. She watches him sit by his teammates.

"I don't know if I can do this." Anna says.

"Forget him. Focus." Casey says throwing the ball to Anna. As Anna shoots a three, Sarah walks in.

"Uh uh. What's she doing here?" Anna asks.

"Beats me." Jenna responds as they watch Sarah approach Al. Anna makes a puking sound as Casey throws her the ball.

"You ready, Anna?" Thomas approaches Anna.

"You know it, ref." Anna responds.

"Let's go!" Joey says approaching them. The game starts, and Anna makes the first point. The whole time the game is going on, Al can't keep his eyes off of Anna. Sarah notices and storms out of the gym.

"You better go get her, Al." One of his teammates laughs.

"I guess you're right." Al leaves go see about Sarah. When Anna sees that, she plays even harder. She goes to win 11 to 8.

"Told you I'd dunk on you." Anna high fives Joey.

"I got mad respect for you, Anna." Joey says. They hug and go to the stands.

"Ready for me?" Will asks.

"You know I am." Anna responds. She rests while the guys shoot around. As soon as Al walks back in, she's ready to play. Anna and Will square off one on one. She almost pulls off the win, but Will steals the ball in mid shot and dunks it for the game winning point.

"Nice try girl." Will says.

"You and Al are the only two I can't beat. Good game, bestie." Anna hugs Will.

"Now, let's clean up and get ready for dinner." Will says. Everyone goes back to the dorm, showers, and dresses up for a nice dinner.

"Y'all clean up nice." Anna says looking at the boys.

"So do you." Joey says as he whistles at Anna.

"I have to take a picture. Anna in a dress and heels?" Will laughs.

"Whatever. Let's go. I'm starving." Anna says.

"Will you be my date tonight?" Joey laughs.

"Why not?" Anna smiles as they walk to Joey's car. When they get to the restaurant, Joey is sitting on Anna's right side with Will and Amber sitting to Anna's left. Jenna and Thomas are across from Anna with Casey and Damen next to them. The last to approach the table is Al and Sarah who sit next to Damen.

"Why is she here?" Anna asks Amber.

"Who knows." Amber shakes her head.

"Al, can you come here dawg?" Joey asks. Al walks over and crouches by Joey's seat.

"What's up?" Al asks.

"What are you doing?" Joey asks.

"Look man. She invited herself. I couldn't just say no. I really don't want her here." Al whispers back.

"You are one dumb brotha." Joey says. Al gets up and goes back to his seat. Anna begins to laugh.

"What's so funny?" Joey asks.

"I heard the whole thing." Anna says.

"Dang nosey." Joey laughs. Al sees Anna and Joey and gets a little jealous. He puts his arm around Sarah to make Anna jealous.

"So, now he's trying to compete." Amber whispers to Anna.

"Ain't nobody got time for him." Anna whispers back.

Once they finish dinner, Joey orders a big cookie with ice cream for him and Anna to share. Thomas and Jenna get one also. Al notices Joey and Anna sharing the cookie, so he asks Sarah to feed him the dessert he ordered. Sarah gets whipped cream on Al's lip and licks it off before he can do it himself.

"Did she just?" Casey asks Anna. Anna simply gets up and leaves the table.

"This has gotten out of hand." Amber says aloud to Al. The girls and Joey go see about Anna. They find her outside crying.

"You okay, Anna?" Amber asks.

"I'm just ready to go. What was he thinking?" Anna barely gets out.

"He's stupid. Forget about him." Jenna says. Joey holds Anna as she cries. Moments later, Al and Sarah walk out. Anna gives him the evil eye and buries her face in Joey's chest. Al feels bad, but does not know what to do. Everyone goes inside to pay their tab, and leaves.

"I'm sorry about Al's behavior." Joey says feeling bad.

"It's cool. It's what I get for falling in love."

"Don't blame yourself for his ignorance."

"Thanks for being here. I appreciate it."

"It's cool. I been knowing Will for a while, and when I met you, I saw you as a sister. So, know I always got your back."

"Thanks." Anna smiles. When they get to the dorm, Anna goes to her room and goes straight to bed.

Al walks Sarah to her dorm.

"You should stay the night." Sarah says.

"Nah. Not tonight. I'm really tired." Al responds.

"What's going on, Al? You keep turning me down. You're in love with Anna, aren't you?"

"What are you talking about? I said I'm tired."

"I've heard about you. I know you're not the type of guy to wait to have sex."

"Look Sarah, I'm just not feeling it. It'll happen when I'm ready. And don't you ever bring up rumors you've heard. They're called rumors for a reason."

"Fine Al. Good night."

"Night. I'll text you when I wake up." Al hugs Sarah and she kisses him on the cheek.

"If you're not gonna give me a real chance, let me know now. I don't deserve to be strung along on a platonic ride." Sarah says looking Al in his eyes. He just walks away without responding.

Will and Joey are in the hall when Al gets to the dorm.

"What's up guys?" Al asks.

"We should be asking you that." Will responds.

"What do you mean?" Al sighs.

"The dinner table tonight. What was Sarah doing there?" Will asks.

"I already told Joey she invited herself." Al answers.

"You know you crossed the line tonight." Joey adds.

"The whipped cream thing? I didn't ask her to do that." Suddenly, Anna opens her door.

"But it never would've happened if you weren't trying to compete. You're so dumb, Al. Jealous of me and Joey?? My brother?? Life would be so much easier for the both of us if you got over yourself! Poor Al. Stuck in a situation he can't get out of. Now, would you keep it down? People are trying to sleep." Anna begins to close her door.

"A situation I can't get out of? I asked Sarah to be my girlfriend tonight. I think you're the one that needs to move on." Al walks down the hall to his room and Anna slams her door.

"This is getting out of control." Joey says as he and Will go to their rooms.

The next morning, Al wakes up questioning what he said to Anna. But, he would look stupid if he really didn't ask Sarah to be his girlfriend. Once dressed, Al goes to walk Sarah to class.

"Morning." Sarah says with an attitude.

"Hey Sarah. I did some thinking about what you said last night. I want you to be my girlfriend."

"What? Are you serious?" Sarah stops dead in her tracks.

"Yes, I am." Al stops and faces her.

"Oh my goodness! I'd love to be your girlfriend!" Sarah jumps in his arms and kisses him.

"I'm glad."

"This is gonna be perfect! The cheerleader and the basketball player." Sarah grabs Al's hand as they walk. Al rolls his eyes, but goes along with it.

Anna goes to the cafeteria with Jenna and Amber for lunch.

"So, what happened last night?" Amber asks.

"Will and Joey were talking to Al in the hallway. I went out there and told it like it was. Called Al a couple names and he called himself hurting my feelings by saying he asked Sarah to be his girlfriend." Anna responds.

"Forreal?" Amber asks.

"I think he said it just to get to me. I can tell he doesn't really like her." Anna says. Moments later, Al and Sarah walk in hand in hand.

"They look together to me." Jenna says Anna doesn't respond. She just stuffs food in her mouth.

"Y'all ready for the season?" Amber asks changing the subject.

"I'm ready to go. I'll catch y'all later." Anna throws her stuff away and leaves.

"I hate seeing her like this." Jenna says.

"Once the season starts, she'll be good." Amber responds as they stare at Sarah and Al.

chapter seven

A couple months pass, and it's finally time for the basketball season to begin. Anna has been so busy focusing on school and basketball, that she barely pays Al any attention. The night before the first home games, Amber and Anna are in Anna's room.

"Ready for the game tomorrow?" Amber asks.

"Hell yeah! I miss the adrenaline rush I feel before every game. It's a feeling like no other." Anna responds.

"You know Sarah's gonna be right on courtside."

"Yeah. She better stay out of my way and hope she doesn't get hit with a ball."

"You're petty." Amber laughs.

"Oh, I know I'm petty. She gon learn today." Anna laughs.

"You staying for the boys' game?"

"Of course. My problem is with Al, not the whole team. You know, all of this drama could've been avoided if men knew how to properly express themselves."

"True! You still love him, don't you?"

"Here's the thing; Al was my first real relationship. On top of that, I fell in love. I don't know if I'm still in love, but feelings are definitely still there. I hate it."

"No matter how much you act like a boy, you're still a girl."

"Ugh. Why couldn't God have made me a guy?"

"Because, if you were a boy, we wouldn't be so cool. That's why." Amber smiles.

"Stop being all mushy." Anna laughs and throws a pillow at Amber.

The next night, Anna is in game mode. As they warm up, Anna sees Sarah on courtside with the rest of the cheerleaders. To be childish, Anna purposely throws the ball too far to the right, hitting Sarah in the back of her head. Anna and Amber crack up laughing. The game starts and Anna plays her heart out as always. People all over the stands call out her name after every shot she makes. Al sits with his teammates watching Anna's every move.

"Make up your mind. Do you want Sarah or Anna?" Damen asks Al. Al looks over at Sarah and notices she sees him looking at Anna. Al quickly focuses back on the game to avoid the awkward situation. The girls go to win the game by ten points.

Thirty minutes later, the guys hit the floor to warm up.

"Good game." Will high fives Anna as they pass each other. Anna and the girls sit and watch the boys warm up. Anna cannot keep her eyes off of Al. After Al shoots a layup, he looks into the stands and makes eye contact with Anna. They both freeze gazing into each other's eyes. Al's gaze is broken when he hears Sarah calling his name in anger. Anna watches with a disappointed look as Al runs to Sarah. She watches Sarah say a few words to Al. Sarah then looks up at Anna and then kisses Al.

"Hold up. Did you and Al just have a moment?" Amber asks.

"I don't know what you're talking about." Anna responds.

"Play dumb if you want. I know what I just saw." Amber smiles.

"It doesn't matter anyways. You saw him run to her like a little puppy when she called him." Anna rolls her eyes. The girls watch the boys win their game by seven points. When the game is over, the girls go to the court.

"Great game." Anna yells as some of the guys come out. As she waits, she sees Al come out. She watches him approach Sarah and kiss her. Anna begins to reminisce about when that was her he kissed after games. Anna's moment is ended when she notices Sarah approaching her.

"Anna." Sarah says.

"What?" Anna asks.

"I know you still love my boyfriend, but can you keep your eyes off of him. It's a distraction to his game."

"Hold up. What?" Anna asks confused.

"You heard me. It was nice chatting with you." Sarah turns to walk away. Anna jumps at Sarah, but Amber holds her back.

"Look here, you're nothing but sloppy seconds! He doesn't really like you! Just wait! He's gonna leave you!" Anna says angrily with Amber still holding her back.

"You sound so jealous. Nobody wants a girl that acts like a guy. That's why he dumped you in the first place." Sarah faces Anna. Anna breaks free from Amber and charges at Sarah.

"Joey stop her!" Amber yells as Joey walks toward them. He quickly steps in Anna's path and grabs her. Al runs over and pulls Sarah from the scene.

"I'm so disappointed in you, Al." Anna shakes her head in disgust. Al just keeps walking out with Sarah.

Joey lets go of Anna once Al and Sarah are gone.

"Don't stoop to their level." Joey says.

"You know I don't tolerate disrespect. Ohh, she's lucky!" Anna storms out of the gym.

"What happened?" Joey asks Amber.

"Sarah just started a war. This has become personal." Amber walks out angrily.

"Will somebody tell me what happened?" Joey asks loudly. One of Anna's teammates fills him in. When the guys get to the dorm, Will and Joey stop at Anna's room.

"You ight, killa?" Will asks Anna.

"I'll be fine. Is Al here? Boy do I have some words for him." Anna says pacing back and forth.

"You need to calm down. Let it go." Joey says.

"Sarah had some nerve tonight!"

"I'm assigning you bodyguards. I know you too well." Will says.

"One of us will be with you at all times until this foolery ends." Joey agrees.

"I can handle myself." Anna says.

"We know. But, you don't want to be suspended from playing ball, do you?" Will asks.

"You're right. I don't even like fighting. That's the angriest I've been since-"

"Sophomore year in high school. Regina." Will finishes Anna's statement.

"Yep. She tried to play you and I tore her up." Anna smirks.

"Sophomore year was so long ago. Let's keep the clean streak going." Will says.

"You're right. She's not worth it." Anna sighs.

The next day in class, Joey and Will sit on both sides of Anna. Al walks in and instantly locks eyes with Anna. After a few seconds, she rolls her eyes and looks away. He feels bad, but doesn't know how to handle the situation.

"You're just digging your grave deeper." Damen says as Al sits down.

The season continues to go on and both teams have outstanding records. Even though Anna is having a great season, it is bittersweet for her. She hates seeing Sarah all over Al after every game. After one of the games in December, the guys take Anna out for her twenty-first birthday.

"Wanna drink?" Joey asks Anna at the restaurant.

"I'm good. I'm not about that life anymore." Anna responds.

"Why not?" Damen asks.

"Over the summer, I realized I only drank to escape my reality. I'm tired of running." Anna says.

"Interesting." Thomas adds.

"I mean, think about it. You drink to make yourself feel good. Why not face whatever stress you're dealing with instead of temporarily relieving yourself?" Anna adds.

"Hmm... well said. I'm proud of you." Will smiles at Anna.

As Anna enjoys her night, things go awry for Al and Sarah as they relax in his room.

"I'm glad to finally be invited over. Where is everybody?" Sarah asks.

"Out for Anna's birthday." Al responds.

"Oh. Is that why you invited me over? Because she's not here?" Sarah asks.

"Here you go again. I'm not about to argue with you."

"I'm sorry. I'm just not used to this. We've been together four months and we barely spend any alone time together. We haven't done more than kiss. I just don't know what to think."

"Is sex all you care about?" Al raises his voice.

"No. But, people tend to want to show affection when they care about each other."

"When I was with Anna, I found out what affection without the physical part meant. Excuse me for not wanting to go back to the old me."

"So, this is about her." Sarah gets angry. Al just gets up and goes to the restroom. Sarah looks around his room and stops at his nightstand. She sees Anna's ring and picks it up in confusion. Moments later, Al comes out of the restroom.

"What the hell is this??" Sarah yells.

"What?"

"Is this the ring you gave Anna? And don't you dare lie."

"It's none of your business."

"The hell it isn't. I'm your girlfriend. Why do you still have this??"

"I can't do this anymore... I still have it because I'm still in love with Anna. I hold that ring every night before I fall asleep. I only got with you to make her jealous."

"You're a pig!" Sarah yells.

"I didn't mean for you to find out this way."

"No. You didn't mean for me to find out at all. I can't believe this!"

"I think you should just leave. It's over between us. I can't do this anymore."

"Wow. You really are a dog. My friends told me not to give you the time of day-"

"It really wasn't my intention to hurt you. But, can you please just leave before you embarrass yourself?"

"Fine. I'm gone! I hate you, Al!" Sarah yells as she knocks a stack of Al's CD's on the ground. Al picks up his CD's and goes to bed not realizing Sarah still has the ring.

The next day, Al doesn't show up to class.

"What's up with your boy? He never skips class." Anna says to Will as they head to the cafeteria. Once they pick a table, Will sees Sarah.

"Mind if I call her over here?" Will asks Anna.

"As long as she doesn't start anything." Anna answers.

"Watch her." Will says to Joey and Amber as he motions to Sarah.

"What's up with Al? He missed class today. That's not like him."

"I don't know. He probably slept in. We had a long night." Sarah smiles.

"Okay thanks." Will says as Sarah pushes her hair away from her face.

"See ya Will." Sarah walks away as Anna's jaw drops.

"Close your mouth." Joey says. Anna is speechless.

"I saw that." Amber says shaking her head.

"Saw what?" Will asks confused.

"That tramp has my ring on." Anna says angrily.

"Seriously?" Joey asks.

"Yes! Now that's just dirty. Al needs to be slapped." Anna throws her food away and storms out.

"Oh lord! Let's go!" Amber exclaims. The three of them throw their trash away and go after Anna.

When they catch up to Anna, she is almost to the dorm.

"What are you doing?" Amber calls out to Anna.

"Giving him what he deserves." Anna storms into her room. Will, Joey, and Amber watch as Anna goes through her drawers pulling out different articles of clothing that belong to Al. Anna grabs the clothes and storms down the hall to Al's room. Joey, Amber, and Will follow at a distance. Holding Al's clothes, Anna kicks Al's door four times.

"What the hell?" Al swings his door open. Anna throws the clothes at him.

"You sick dog! Here's every bit of you I tried to hold on to!" Anna yells. Guys peak out of their rooms.

"What??" Al yells snatching the clothes off of himself.

"You gave that tramp my promise ring!! That's the lowest thing I've ever seen you do. I'm disgusted just looking at you."

"What are you talking about??" Al raises his voice.

"Are you stupid? Your girlfriend has my promise ring on!"

"I broke up with her last night! I don't even know why she has it!"

"So, we're lying now? Whatever Al. Go to hell. I never wanna see your face again!" Anna storms out of the dorm, and Amber follows. All of Al's teammates stare at him.

"What are y'all lookin' at??" Al slams his door.

Amber runs after Anna.

"Anna! Are you okay??" Amber yells. Anna stops and falls to her knees. Will runs outside and sees Anna. He runs to her and takes her in his arms.

"I don't wanna be here anymore." Anna cries.

"Everything's gonna be alright." Amber says feeling bad. Will sees Al storm out of the dorm. Al doesn't look their way. When he makes it to Sarah's dorm, he bangs on her door.

"Hello??" Sarah asks with an attitude.

"What did you do??" Al yells.

"Whatever could you be talking about?" Sarah smirks.

"Give me the ring!"

"Why should I? So you can be happily ever after with her?? I don't think so. If I can't have you, neither can Anna." Sarah raises her voice.

"Why would you do something like that?"

"I wanted her to hurt like I was. Now you can't have either of us." Sarah explains. Al grabs Sarah's arm and pulls the ring off. Sarah tries to fight it, but Al is too strong.

"You're gonna apologize!"

"The hell I am!"

"I'll be back, and you better have your speech ready!" Al storms off.

"Whatever Al!" Sarah slams her door.

Joey is waiting for Al in the dorm.

"Al, what's going on, man?" Joey asks.

"Sarah took the ring after I broke up with her last night... I still love Anna." Al confides.

"It took four months to realize that? You've driven her to the point of no return." Joey says.

"Don't say that, man. I gotta get her back." Al says. Joey just walks to his room shaking his head.

The next day in class, Anna sits in a corner far away from Al. She cannot believe things have come to this.

"Will, you gotta help me win her back." Al says desperately.

"I want nothing to do with this." Will responds.

"Come on dawg. You know me. Yeah, I was childish for dating Sarah, but you know I didn't give her that ring." Al tries to convince Will.

"Fine. You come up with your plan, and I'll get her to the location. You're lucky you're my boy, or else I'd never vouch for you." Will says.

"Thanks Will. We can come up with an idea this weekend while we're away." Al smiles. The upcoming weekend, both teams have away games. The guys help Al come up with something romantic for Anna.

When both teams get back to school, the plan goes into full effect on a cold, snowy night. Anna is alone in her room until Will and Amber walk in.

"What's up guys?" Anna asks.

"Get dressed." Will demands.

"For what? No. It's cold outside." Anna argues.

"Anna, don't be difficult. Can you please come on? It's not gonna take long." Amber reinforces.

"Fine. I'm gonna be really upset if this is for something silly." Anna throws on her winter gear and the three of them head outside. Will and Amber lead Anna to the place Al asked Anna to be his girl.

"Can you walk a little faster?" Will asks Anna.

"Look negro, I didn't wanna come in the first place." Anna says with an attitude. Suddenly, the area lights up with Christmas lights in Anna's favorite colors. Anna looks around amazed.

"We're just gonna stay back here in case she does something crazy." Will says quietly to Amber as Anna keeps walking forward.

"Good idea." Amber agrees. Anna continues to observe the lights as Al approaches her with a red rose and a cup of hot chocolate.

"What are you doing here?" Anna asks with an attitude.

"I set this up for you."

"So, you think some pretty lights and a rose is gonna win me over? Think again."

"Can you please just hear me out for a few minutes?" Al asks handing Anna the hot chocolate.

"Fine. You have five minutes." Anna says.

"Okay... I am so sorry for everything that's happened over the past four months. I was hurt and I handled it the wrong way."

"Ya think?" Anna rolls her eyes.

"I only got with Sarah to make you jealous. I thought something was going on between you and Joey."

"But why?"

"Y'all were all laughing and sharing dessert. And I didn't invite Sarah. She shows up at my truck as I'm leaving and tells me she's coming."

"Mhm. What about the licking off of the whipped cream?"

"She just did that. I didn't have anything to do with it."

"You let it happen!"

"Everything just went downhill from there. I haven't been happy since you and I broke up. I've been trying to fill a void that only you can fill." Al says ignoring Anna's last statement.

"What about the ring?"

"She found it on your birthday. That's when I broke up with her. I was so upset I didn't realize she kept it."

"B.S."

"I'm telling the truth! You of all people should know better."

"I don't know you anymore. This whole time you've been doing things I never thought you'd do."

"Anna... I love you."

"It took you this long to figure that out?" There is a long pause, "Bye Al. I don't love you anymore." Anna hands him the rose and leaves. Will and Amber approach Al.

"I'm sorry bro." Will says as Al takes out the new ring he bought her.

"That's beautiful." Amber says.

"Yeah." Al walks back to the dorm with his head down.

A couple weeks pass, and Al still wants Anna back.

"I don't know what to do, man." Al tells Will during practice.

"Have you talked to Sarah?"

"A while ago. She won't talk to Anna."

"There has to be some type of incentive for her." Will says.

"Do you still have those pictures from that Omega party last year??" Al asks.

"I sure do. That's why you my dawg." Once practice is over, Will gets the pictures and Al heads to Sarah's dorm. Twenty minutes later, Al and Sarah knock on Anna's door.

"You've got some nerve bringing her here. What do you want?" Anna asks with an attitude. Will, Joey, and Amber eavesdrop from Will's room.

"Sarah has something to tell you." Al says. Sarah rolls her eyes.

"I'm listening." Anna says angrily.

"Fine! I took the ring! I wanted you to think he gave it to me. If I couldn't have him, I didn't want you to have him either."

"But, why? I told you your place last time you tried something."

"I was hurt. Hell, I still am. But, I realize I took it too far... So, he's all yours."

"Was that an apology?" Anna asks.

"I'm sorry for everything, Anna."

"Apology accepted. You can leave now. I don't ever wanna see you talking to him. Don't wave, hell, don't even look at him." Anna orders.

"Whatever." Sarah leaves. Anna just stares at Al.

"You don't want her looking at me? So does that mean we're back together?" Al asks.

"Not quite. First, I must apologize again for shutting you out. But, I need to know you won't step out on me if something else drastic happens between us."

"I promise! The past four months without you were miserable!"

"Question: did y'all do anything?"

"Other than kiss, no. I couldn't do it. Being with you made me realize that I don't need sex to have a great relationship." Al says. Anna jumps in Al's arms and kisses him.

"I missed you!" Anna smiles.

"Not as much as I missed you!" Al reaches in his pocket and hands a box to Anna.

"What is it?"

"Open it." Al says as Anna opens the box.

"It's beautiful! Thank you! Sorry for being a jerk." Anna says putting the ring on.

"It's fine. I was one, too."

"Oh yeah, I want your clothes back."

"The ones you threw at me? I gotchu." Al smiles and kisses Anna. Will, Joey, and Amber open Will's door and start cheering. Al turns him and Anna around and they both start laughing.

"Weirdos." Anna says as Al carries her to his room.

"I hated sleeping alone." Al says once they get to his room.

"I did too. But, we do have to discuss something."

"What about?"

"I don't think we should be sleeping in the same bed anymore. Keeping my virginity means a lot to me, and I don't want to jeopardize it. It's not that I don't trust you, I just don't want to leave any room for error."

"I should've known this was coming."

"I hope you understand. Spending that week with my granny really changed my life. She brought some things to my attention that made a lot of sense. With that being said, I think it is very important for the both of us to remain pure if we want this relationship to last."

"You're right. So, that means no being in the same bed... ever?"

"Ever. Until I am legally Mrs. Peters."

"I understand. I'm down. It's not gonna be easy, but I'm willing to do whatever to make this work."

"I love you." Anna hugs Al.

"Thought you didn't love me anymore."

"I lied." Anna smiles.

"I love you too." Al smiles back. The two of them sit in Al's room and catch up.

That weekend, both teams have back to back home games. Everyone is shocked to see Anna and Al walk in hand in hand. The girls win their game, as they have every home game. As the boys begin to warm up, Anna kisses Al for good luck and goes to her seat next to Monica and Amie.

"I'm glad you and Al are back together." Monica says.

"Me too." Anna responds smiling hard. Once the guys finish their game, the girls, along with Monica and Amie, go to the court. As soon as Anna sees Al, she runs and jumps in his arms.

"Great game baby!" Anna says.

"Thanks. You too."

"I missed this."

"Me too. I love you."

"I love you too." Al kisses Anna as everyone including Amie and Monica cheer. As Al predicted, he got his girl back.